CHRISTMAS WITH A CHIMERA

ISABELLE TAYLOR

CONTENT WARNINGS

On-page sex, knotting.

Kindle eBook ASIN: B0DHY1L9W8

KDP Paperback ISBN: 979-8-342814-26-3

IngramSpark Paperback ISBN: 978-1-067014-17-9

IngramSpark Hardcover ISBN: 978-1-067014-18-6

ONE

"Huh," said Arthur Pineclaw as the limo cruised into town. "They changed the sign."

Rusty didn't look up from his phone. The director had been exceedingly dull since they got off their Los Angeles to Alaska flight, spending most of the limo ride on his phone.

Arthur extended a wing and nudged the human. "Rust. They changed it."

Rusty glanced up. "What? Oh. Yeah, bud, I bet a lot's changed. How long has it been since you came back?"

"Over a decade." Arthur shot him a bright smile to cover up the nerves squirming in his stomach and peered out the window again. "It can't have changed *that* much. You know our movie theater only had one studio, and they'd play one movie for six months?"

"Times are a-changing," Rusty said, shoving his phone in his pocket. "Your hometown's a big draw for tourists nowadays. We're lucky the location scouts thought of it. *And* that they let us film. You know the Cozy Grotto Cafe?"

"Nope. Must've rebranded." Arthur stared out at the town as it came into view. The streets were shockingly less shabby than he remembered. Crowded, too. Gone were the dingy Christmas decorations Arthur had grown up with; now, they had brand-new lights winding up lampposts and shiny wreaths hanging off every door. Some of them were even monster-themed, which Arthur got a kick out of.

Claw Haven, the new sign had declared. *For the monster who wants some peace and quiet.* It was a cute little slogan. Arthur might have even liked it if he was the kind of guy who enjoyed peace and quiet.

But Arthur was meant for cityscapes and noise. Which was why he got out of this sleepy town the year after high school ended and hadn't looked back since. Not until Rusty got in touch with an exciting new opportunity: a Christmas rom-com based in Arthur's own hometown.

We don't want to do it without you, Rusty had told him after his agent put them in touch. *If you don't say yes, we might as well scrap the whole project.*

So, of course, Arthur had signed on. How could he not with so many people counting on him? Besides, he'd been meaning to squeeze another shoot into his winter schedule. It was a quick enough job: they'd already shot in LA for a month, and now they needed two weeks in

Claw Haven for the small-town scenes. They'd wrap on Christmas Eve, and Arthur would be back in LA in time for another carefree Christmas watching the holiday episodes of *Friends,* eating takeout, and "forgetting" to call his parents, who would in turn "forget" to call him before trading apologies and promising a New Year's call that would never happen.

Rusty tapped on the partition. "Driver! Cozy Grotto Cafe, we're here!"

The limo skidded to a stop outside a cafe that Arthur vaguely remembered. It used to be called something different, but it had still been a cafe. One of the *only* cafes. Not anymore, though—they'd multiplied since Arthur had gone. He counted at least four tucked in between the revamped bookstore, bakery, and tattoo studio. They even had a *skincare* shop now, which was exciting. He only had so many of his special creams, and he could already feel his mane drying out.

Arthur slipped his sunglasses on and turned to Rusty. "I can pull these off, right? They're not too much?"

"You look great," Rusty assured him. He clapped Rusty on the back, right between his wings. "Ready for your triumphant return?"

"Always." Arthur winked, telling his pesky nerves to shut up. He had nothing to be nervous about. He was popular in high school, and now he was returning as a movie star. He had a *limo*, for god's sake. These small-town folks wouldn't know what hit them.

He shook out his mane and climbed out onto the snowy sidewalk. A few shoppers glanced his way, one of them even did a double take. But no mobs, no pleading for autographs. Arthur told himself he was relieved. He liked the attention, but it got tiring sometimes.

Rust shivered. "Goddamn! This cold is *intense*. Wish *I* had fur."

"We can't all be perfect," Arthur told him, stretching out his cramped wings. First a plane ride, then a limo ride —he would need a good fly around while he was here. Even if it didn't stop snowing, it was manageable to fly in. He used to do it all the time. A million years ago, back when he spent every winter flying around the mountains with a certain someone's arms around his shoulders, her bright laugh in his ear...

He squeezed his eyes shut. One thing he had decided when he told Rusty he'd do the movie: this wasn't a trip down memory lane. He had a script from his publicist about what to say in interviews, but those were all vague and mostly fake. He wasn't going to get lost in the memories. *Especially* not memories about her.

He reached for the cafe door.

It swung open, a peppy human beaming up at him. Her hair was blonde and glossy, her clothes the kind of fashionable he thought you couldn't get in Claw Haven.

"Hi," she said, her accent decidedly *not* local. "I'm Luna Musgrove!"

"You're the one who reached out to my agent and got Rusty on board," he supplied, stepping past her into the warm cafe. It was bigger than he'd expected, all tiny tables and ornate chairs and a persistent smell of cinnamon in the air. A camera guy was setting up near the counter, and a prop guy slotting plastic minotaur-themed cupcakes into the cabinet.

Arthur turned toward the door, calling out into the cold. "Rusty! It's your old pal, Luna!"

Rusty rushed into the cafe after him, brushing snow out of his hair. "Luna, hi. Great to finally meet you in person. You look even better off Zoom."

"Aw, so do you." Luna kissed his cheek. "*So* glad you're here. There are some set people out back who have a ton of questions for you, something to do with lighting."

"On it," Rusty said and took off in the direction Luna was pointing.

Luna brushed her blonde strands out of her face. She was definitely from LA; he was sure of it now—she had that *look*. Dentist-perfect teeth and glowing skin. She looked chic and adorable in her puffy winter clothes, which were much thicker than anything a local would wear. This was a woman who wasn't used to the Alaskan cold.

"Jennifer's still in makeup," Luna told him. "She's excited to see you."

"Jen's a firecracker," Arthur said, another thing his publicist had supplied. "I've really been enjoying our shoot."

Unlike many things his publicist had him say, both of

these statements were true. Jen *was* a firecracker—fun, impulsive, and loud. She was human and a few years younger than him, and the more time he spent with her, the more he got the feeling she'd like to be more than costars. But that was a thought for another day. He didn't like getting involved with his costars until they finished filming. That way they weren't stuck together five days a week if something went sideways. He learned *that* the hard way.

"So," he said. "You're the girl who revitalized the town."

Luna shrugged happily. "I just showed them what was already there. Claw Haven did the rest."

Arthur doubted it. The town's abrupt shift from boring snooze-fest to cute, cozy monster town didn't happen by accident. He'd only seen one street, but he could tell how different it was. Whatever Luna had done, she might've actually turned it into someplace worthwhile. For a visit, anyway.

"Where are you from?" he asked. "You sound like an LA woman."

Luna curtsied. "Born and raised!"

"And you live *here*? Voluntarily?"

Luna laughed. "What can I say? It has its charm."

"Now, maybe." Arthur looked out the cafe's frosted windows at the bustling street, which was more crowded than he'd ever seen it. "I couldn't do it. I'd miss the city too much."

"I miss it sometimes," Luna said easily. "But I got so

attached to this place. It's small, it's close-knit—everybody knows you."

"For better or worse."

"Just gotta make sure it's for the better." Luna smiled again, soft and warm. She wasn't looking at him anymore —she was staring into the distance, twisting her wedding ring around her finger.

All at once, Arthur understood. She'd moved here for a guy. Some poor schmuck that Arthur probably knew from high school. And in her boredom, Luna had decided to actually do something with the town to make it worth living in. Not bad work. Now she just needed to make it a hundred times bigger and move it somewhere warm. He hoped the guy wasn't too upset when she gave up on this place and moved to brighter pastures.

A personal assistant came by with a wonky headset and the glazed look of someone who had been awake for far too long.

"Coffee orders," the PA asked, a pen poised over a raggedy notebook.

"Just a latte," Luna said breezily.

"Same for me," Arthur said. He had a usual coffee order that included caramel shots and two kinds of milk, but he was trying to be gracious. He didn't want to confuse these small-town baristas.

Somebody laughed. Arthur turned to see a young minotaur woman and a human woman come in from the backrooms, both of them dressed in white shirts and aprons.

"Still weird that we're sending them off to get coffee,"

the minotaur woman was saying. "We have a coffee machine right..."

She trailed off. Her eyes went wide on Arthur, who beamed. *There* was the starstruck look he was waiting for. Except the longer he looked at it, the less he was sure her furry face was starstruck. She looked... concerned?

The human, however, gasped. "Oh my god! That's Arthur Pineclaw! Daisy, wasn't I literally *just* saying how cool it would be if it was him?"

"Yeah," Daisy said slowly, her soft nose twitching. "So... cool."

Luna gestured at them. "Arthur! This is Daisy and Hazel. They're a couple of the staff, and they'll be extras during the cafe scenes."

Arthur waved. He didn't recognize either of them. They both looked younger; they might have been in middle school when he was in high school. Or maybe they had moved here since he left—apparently, Claw Haven was the place to be nowadays. According to Rusty, they'd had more people move here in the last few years than in the entire time his parents lived here.

"You look surprised," he told them. "Didn't Luna tell you it was me?"

Both girls shook their heads.

"Rusty wanted it to be a surprise," Luna said brightly.

The minotaur still looked worried, which Arthur was determinedly not taking as a bad omen. Maybe she just got really anxious around movie stars. She'd probably never met one before. Nobody important stopped in Claw Haven—at least not while he was growing up.

Hazel, the human, looked delighted. "It makes sense now that I think about it, though. You've been in a bunch of rom-coms, right?"

"Sure have!" He grinned. "Rom-coms have sadly fallen to the wayside lately. We're trying to bring them back."

"Well, if anyone can do it, it's you," Hazel gushed. She tugged on Daisy's furry arm. "I can't believe the boss agreed to this! Luna, you should've mentioned it was Arthur Pineclaw; I bet she would've agreed *way* faster."

"Ha ha ha," Daisy said, too loud. "Totally. Hey Luna, can I talk to you for a second?"

Luna blinked, startled by her tone. "Sure! What's up?"

"Alone," Daisy said.

"Sure," Luna said after a beat. She turned to Arthur, blonde ponytail bouncing. "I'll just be one moment. Toodles!"

"Toodles," Arthur replied. He watched them head out of the cafe: Luna rubbing her arms despite her thick jacket, Daisy giving him an awkward nod as she followed her out. They immediately bent their heads together, Daisy speaking quietly and urgently.

Weird, he thought. Maybe Daisy had a problem with him. Whatever it was, he was sure he could charm her into liking him before the shoot was over. They had two weeks. There weren't a lot of people who could withstand Arthur's charm for two weeks without at least *grudgingly* liking him. Still, it was a surprise: he hadn't run into many people who openly disliked him for a long time. Not since he'd become a movie star, anyway.

Hazel slunk up to him with a shy, excited look that he was *much* more familiar with.

He beamed, twisting his whiskers rakishly. "Would you like an autograph?"

"Yes!" She dug in her apron and produced a biro and a wrinkled notebook. He scribbled his name with a flourish, adding a heart and Hazel's name underneath. She seemed like the kind of girl who'd appreciate a personal touch.

Hazel giggled, slipping the signed notebook and pen back into her apron. "Thank you! This is so cool. I love *Just Kitten Around*. And that mermaid one— What was that called?"

"*In Too Deep*," Arthur said.

Hazel clapped. "Yes! *In Too Deep* made me cry!"

"Always great to meet a fan," Arthur said, watching Daisy and Luna out of the corner of his eye. Luna's smile was stiff with concealed panic, which wasn't making him feel any more at ease. He might have his work cut out for him with that minotaur.

He flexed his wings and turned back to Hazel. "So! Who's your boss? I bet I know them."

"I bet you do," Hazel said, blushing under the full force of his award-winning smile. "You two probably went to high school together, now that I think about it. You're about the same age."

"Oh?" Arthur asked, interest piqued. "Don't keep me in suspense. Who is it?"

"Her name is—" Hazel stopped, head cocking. "Oh, that's her now! Don't tell her I got an autograph; she told me not to bother you."

A low, angry mutter was coming from the back.

I know that pissed-off mutter, Arthur thought with growing disbelief. Even with everything screaming inside him that it couldn't be her—why would she buy a *cafe*?—he knew. He'd recognize her voice anywhere.

The back doors flew open. A woman charged through, clutching a bag of coffee beans.

"Fancy pants think they own the place," she muttered, absentmindedly stopping a coffee bean from toppling out the open end of the bag. "Putting shit in *our* fridges—"

She looked up, coming to a sudden halt.

Hazel waved. "Hey, boss! Look who's here! Blast from the past, right?"

The woman didn't respond. She was staring at him, her arms slack around the bag of coffee beans.

Arthur swallowed with a suddenly dry throat. Her hair was shorter: once it hung under her shoulders. Now it was a pixie cut, frazzled and wispy over her forehead. She was wearing a Christmas sweater so tacky that Arthur ached to tweak the snowman's beady nose like he would've done all those years ago.

"Emma," he said, as charming as he could muster. "Great to see you again."

Emma Curt gaped at him. Despite everything,

Arthur's heart squeezed painfully in his chest. Once, he'd believed this woman would be the rest of his life. Now she was staring at him like she was offended he was breathing her air. Annoyed and gorgeous, just the way he'd left her.

"What the fuck is he doing here?" she demanded. Then she grimaced. "Oh, shit."

Her arms tightened, but it was too late: the coffee bag slipped through her hands and crashed to the floor.

Two

Emma stared at the coffee beans scattered all over the cafe floor.

She wanted to be more annoyed about it. But her anger was frustratingly distant, even as she realized that beans must've fallen under the counter again, and they'd have to do something about that after the damn film crew left.

It was hard to feel anything but complete and utter shock.

Arthur Pineclaw. Here. Now. In *her* fucking cafe. Smiling at her like butter wouldn't melt in his mouth. His mane was perfectly coiffed and shiny, his fangs gleaming. He was wearing sunglasses indoors, like an asshole.

She watched in stunned silence as Arthur bent down and plucked a single coffee bean between his claws.

"Well," he announced. "One down."

There was the anger Emma had been looking for. She glared at him, this pompous jackass who thought he could skate through life on charm and charisma. And infuriatingly enough, it *worked*.

Emma squared her shoulders. That might help Arthur in LA, but it wasn't going to help him in Cozy Grotto Cafe. Not with Emma in charge.

"No one's answering my question," she said. "What the fuck is he doing here?"

The guy who had been setting up the camera slunk toward the backroom. Emma ignored him, still glaring at her employee.

"Um," squeaked Hazel, who was looking even more unprepared than usual. Hazel was sweet but a bit of a ditz. She couldn't make coffee to save her life. Emma would've fired her months ago if Hazel wasn't so damn determined to learn. Still, Emma had come close more than a few times. It was hard to defend her against the tenth complaining tourist of the day, and Emma often wondered why she bothered.

"He's the actor guy," Hazel said weakly. "The one Luna was talking about?"

"Great," Emma snapped. "Just as helpful as always, Hazel. Thanks for nothing."

Hazel wilted. Emma had a moment of guilt before the cafe door swung open.

Luna and Daisy rushed in, Daisy looking apologetic, and Luna with that giant smile that Emma was growing wary of. She didn't trust anyone who smiled that much. Case in point: her movie star ex, who was still holding that stupid coffee bean as if he was actually helping.

"Em," Luna said like she could squash the rancid

vibes with the sheer force of her peppy tone. "You're here! Great! This is Arthur. Daisy was just telling me that you two know each other—"

"Yeah, no shit." Emma blinked hard. Her eyes were burning. What the hell? She wasn't going to *tear up* just because her high school sweetheart was back in town.

"I'm not doing this," she decided and headed for the door. "Hazel, could you tidy this up?"

"Got it," Hazel blurted, stepping around the coffee beans to grab the broom propped up behind the counter. She almost skidded on a bean, but luckily, Daisy rushed over to steady her.

"Em," Luna tried. "Hold up a second."

Arthur made a noise like he was going to say something. He even reached out with his stupid bean-holding hand.

Emma whirled on him, growling. She was fully human, even her sharpest teeth were woefully blunt, but she could still make some impressive noise. It was enough to make Arthur stop.

He stared at her, smile dropping. His hand flexed in the empty air, and Emma's stomach twisted with heat as she remembered that same hand stroking over her bare body, curling inside her, touching the place where he was swollen inside her—

She turned back to the door. She wasn't going to lust after the chimera who broke her heart, no matter how long it had been since she went to bed with someone, let alone let anyone *knot* her.

She marched out into the busy street with Luna behind her. Freezing wind stung her cheeks.

"Em," Luna tried again. "I'm so sorry, the director said it should be a surprise!"

Emma spun to face her, dragging them out of the stream of Christmas shoppers who had burst onto the scene. Thanks to Luna Musgrove, Claw Haven's tourist population increased a thousandfold in the last few years.

"They need to use another cafe," Emma announced. "We have a bunch now! Pick one!"

She waved her arms, indicating all the cafes tucked between the chocolate shop, the flower shop, the bakery, the bookshop, and that goddamn skincare shop, which always kept the sign out overnight despite Emma constantly telling the old woman who owned it to bring it in before someone stole it or defaced it. *Then* some-one's dumb teenager stole it and returned it with several of the sign's letters blacked out to spell a word that none of them wanted to be affiliated with.

Luna sighed. "So, unfortunately, you've already signed the contract—"

"Fuck the contract!" Emma said, loud enough that two passing harpies glanced over. Then they saw who they were looking at and wisely looked away. Nobody wanted to be on Emma Curt's bad side.

"You didn't say it was him," Emma continued. "I was expecting some B-list minotaur who made a bunch of fur care adverts! If I'd known, I would *never*—"

She stopped, throat closing up. She averted her eyes, scrubbing her thankfully dry cheeks. She wasn't about to cry in front of Luna Musgrove, who was a friend but *definitely* not someone Emma wanted to cry in front of. She only did that in front of her parents, who had seen far worse. Besides, Luna looked like she would rather throw herself into traffic than watch her cry, which was coincidentally also what Emma was feeling.

Then Luna's panicked smile turned soft. She took a deep breath, reaching up to squeeze Emma's arm.

"Nope," Emma blurted.

"Still no touching, okay!" Luna held her hands up in surrender. "Let's get some coffee."

Emma sniffed. "Some assistant guy is bringing me an iced coffee."

"Right. I forgot you're one of those people who drink iced coffee in this weather." Luna dragged her puffy jacket tighter. "They'll give it to the crew. Come on, my treat."

Emma considered. It was this or go back to the cafe —and she couldn't face him again. She needed time to get her head on straight, to—

She stopped, staring behind them at a long, sleek vehicle parked in front of Cozy Grotto Cafe.

"Is that a *limo*?" she asked disbelievingly.

Luna twisted to look at it. "Guess so. Seems like a fellow drama queen."

"You have no idea," Emma muttered.

A cold breeze blew through the street, making Luna shudder and Emma sigh. Luna was from California, so she spent most of the coldest months with her werewolf husband around, ready to duck into his arms and get warm. Even with all those layers, her teeth started chattering if she stayed out in the cold for more than thirty seconds.

"Fine," Emma grumbled. "Let's go before you turn into a popsicle."

They picked a corner table in Creature Comforts. Other than her own cafe, it was the only cafe on Main Street that did iced coffees the way Emma wanted them: no ice cubes, extra whipped cream on top, and extra chocolate sauce.

Luna nibbled on a minotaur-shaped chocolate that came with her drink. Prickles, the hedgehog-owned chocolate shop, was yet another business that was booming thanks to Luna's marketing expertise. Emma had to give it to her: turning Prickles into the supplier for all the local cafes' chocolate needs was a smart move. Stellar chocolate, too. She'd gotten more than a little addicted to all these little goodies that came with her coffees.

"I really am sorry," Luna said as she nibbled. "Daisy gave me the short version before you came in. Sounds like there's some tricky history there."

Emma laughed bitterly. "You could say that."

Luna dropped the rest of her chocolate into her latte and leaned forward. She had that coy smile on, the one that made it easy to believe that she'd been the go-to girl to spice up a party back in LA. She still did the same in Claw Haven, but she usually tapped out with her werewolf husband before too long. Emma was surprised that he wasn't around. They'd renewed their wolf bond at their wedding, and it usually meant that they had to keep each other on a short leash or risk an impressive amount of pain—for a while, anyway. Apparently, it had been longer than Emma thought.

Emma braced herself. "We dated in high school."

Luna nodded eagerly. "And?"

"Stop looking like you're watching reality TV," Emma scolded. "This is my *life*."

"Right," Luna said. "Sorry."

Emma leaned back in her chair, folding her arms tightly over her chest. Arthur used to tease her for it and show her how to look more relaxed. *You catch more flies with honey*, he used to say. He probably still said it. It sounded like the stupid sort of thing he'd say, convinced that all of life could be solved if you hid everything behind a bullshit smile.

"That's the whole story," Emma said. "We dated in high school. He abandoned me to be a movie star. Looks like it worked out for him."

She sucked whipped cream off her spoon grudgingly. She'd buy a can of Cool Whip on her way home, she decided. It was a night for old movies and eating Cool Whip straight from the can. The kind of night where she convinced herself she was fucking *ecstatic* with her life instead of just content. She had never expected to end up owning a cafe, but she'd been getting bored of her managerial job at the supermarket and the cafe owner was thinking of shutting down, and

Emma didn't want to switch to instant coffee. So she took out a loan and bought the place. It turned out she was pretty damn good at running a cafe, especially when Luna swaggered in and changed everything. Nowadays, the cafe wasn't just scraping by, they were *thriving*. Just like Emma, who was *completely* happy with her life, no matter what her parents said. She didn't need a partner. She'd sworn off serious relationships after the debacle with Arthur. She had friends, a great job, and a *purpose*, even if that purpose was making sure people had enough energy to make it through the morning. Arthur could take his big-city life and shove it up his furry ass.

Luna asked, "Were you engaged?"

"No!" Emma scoffed. "We were *eighteen*. Nineteen, I guess. We spent a year stacking shelves at the Ghoulish Grocer. It wasn't enough for him."

She dug her spoon into her iced chocolate, stirring savagely. She could tell Luna more—that he never proposed, they never talked about a wedding. But they talked about their future all the time. They even had a house picked out: small and sweet, near the middle of town. He always said he'd do it up. Give it some fresh paint and fix the porch. He said he'd grow wisteria and they could sit out on that fixed-up wraparound porch when they had their morning coffees. She could sit on his lap. He'd close his wings around her to keep her warm, as he did so often in their teenage years. They'd almost had enough for the deposit. Arthur's parents were going to help them out. They were only a few months away from talking to the bank when Arthur ambushed her on that Christmas walk.

All along, that house had been a lie. He'd had his eyes set on city life ever since they visited during summer break junior year. She hated it upon arrival, but he'd fallen in love. He'd tried to talk her into moving there with him, but she held fast. Eventually, he stopped bringing it up. She thought he was happy here.

Maybe it's better this way. You won't be holding me back anymore. Those were his parting words before he climbed into the taxi his parents had paid for and left her life forever.

She'd really thought it was forever. She'd heard the gossip around town after his first leading role in a bartender rom-com called *Whisker Neat*. She'd even ripped down a few photographs they'd hung up around her old high school, Arthur's beaming face photoshopped to high hell in whatever movie he was in this time. His parents moved away a few years after he became successful. There was no reason for him to come back to Claw Haven.

Then she'd walked into her cafe and found him standing there in his fancy suit and insufferable sunglasses. There had been a second of shock, she was sure of it; a trace of genuine emotion slipping through the facade. Then he'd smiled at her like she was just another person in the neverending list of people he could trick into liking him.

Once, she was the only person he could be real around. Now she wasn't even that. She was *nothing*.

"Look," Luna said, that soft look overtaking her unstoppable interest in gossip. "Everything's gonna be fine. You're already getting paid, you don't even need to be there!"

Emma sucked on her iced coffee resentfully. "Like hell. If people are doing shit in my cafe, I'm going to be there. They were messing with the fridges! The fridges aren't going to be in the scene!"

"I'll tell Rusty to make them lay off the fridges," Luna said soothingly.

"You'd better." Emma folded her arms tighter, doing her best not to think about how Arthur used to unfold them for her and tangle their fingers together, his long fingers fitting perfectly between hers.

There, he'd always say, curling his wings around her to form a safe, all-encompassing shelter that once felt like it took up the whole world. *Now you look like the kind of person a guy can walk up and say hello to.*

"It's just a few weeks," Luna pointed out. "Then you'll never have to see him again."

A throat cleared behind them.

Emma stiffened. She was already scowling before she turned to find Arthur Pineclaw standing next to their table, those absurd sunglasses perched up in his mane. He had *laugh lines.* The sight of them sent a white-hot rage through her stomach, curdling her iced coffee. How *dare* he look so hot without Photoshop?

"Emma," he said with another ridiculous red-carpet smile. "We should talk."

THREE

A rthur should've seen it coming.

The humming. The fake-consideration. Emma even scratched her chin the same way she did when she was preparing to tear someone to shreds when they were teenagers.

"Go to hell," she told him. She took a large sip of what he assumed was iced coffee, because, of course, she still enjoyed freezing drinks in the depths of Alaskan winter. "Or should I say go to LA? Same thing. Sorry," she added to Luna.

Luna laughed, twirling her wedding ring. "No offense taken! City life isn't for everybody."

"Right," Arthur agreed. "Some people prefer places where everybody you walk past knows what you did at a party last Friday, and there's nowhere to get sushi if you have a 3 a.m. craving."

Emma threw up her hands. "Make some macaroni! Ugh. I *knew* you'd get worse down there. Do you have

someone to do your laundry? Does someone come to
your house and clip your claws for you? Do you have
your own wing-groomer?"

Arthur flexed his wings uncomfortably. He had a
different guy for all three of those things. In his defense,
he was a very busy chimera.

Luna pushed her chair back. "And that's my cue! Em,
I'll see you tomorrow?"

Emma grumbled something so low Arthur didn't
hear it. But she shrugged, taking another annoyed sip of
iced coffee.

"Great," Luna said brightly. "See you both tomorrow!"

She flounced off, pulling her puffy jacket tight
around her as she ducked back into the cold.

Arthur turned back to Emma, who was folding her
arms tightly over her Christmas sweater.

Arthur twitched with the urge to pry them apart.
The intensity of it surprised him. He hadn't thought
about that in years: coaxing Emma's soft side out,
nuzzling her cheek, and joking with her until she finally
relented. Her parents, for some strange reason, had taken
a while to warm up to him. But watching him make her
smile like that, all relaxed and giddy, was the thing that
finally made them approve. Once, he'd been the only
person who could pull Emma out of a truly terrible
mood. Who could make her put down her snappish ways
and admit what was really bothering her. Who could
tease a laugh out of her even when she was raging. Now...

"Nice Christmas sweater," he said.

She scowled. "You finally admit it! You always thought they were cute, you were just too chicken to wear them in case people *judged* you. Newsflash, Christmas sweaters are *adorable*. Asshole."

Arthur held back a smile. Same old Emma. Any time she felt an emotion she didn't like, she buried it under a tidal wave of anger. It made sense that seeing him again would trigger all this scowling. He just had to dig deeper to get to the real stuff, like he used to.

Her gaze dropped toward his pants. "Thought you were working on that."

"Working on what?"

She pointed. He looked down to see his tail... *moving*. A barely-there back and forth as if swaying in a breeze.

Arthur fought back a wince. Tails were usually a dead giveaway for whatever the monster it was attached to was feeling. He prided himself on having an unusually still tail, only moving when a scene called for it.

He stilled it with a gracious laugh. "Down, boy. Thank you, I didn't even notice. Must be Claw Haven—old habits."

"Right," Emma said suspiciously. Still glaring. Still crossing her arms over her chest so tight that the snowman looked like it was being strangled.

Arthur tried again. "How are your parents?"

"Fine," Emma said stiffly. She hesitated. For a moment, Arthur thought she was going to give him more details, and he found himself surprisingly eager to hear them. He always liked her parents. He'd seen them more than his own parents in his teenage years.

"I'm gonna go," Emma said instead.

She stood up, chair scraping noisily.

Before he could think better of it, he stepped in front of her, blocking her exit.

She rolled her eyes. "Move."

He briefly thought about extending his wings, then noticed how many tables and chairs he'd knock over if he did. One thing winged monsters were taught young: don't get your wings out inside unless you're really, *really* careful.

"You always did love telling me no," he mused.

"Somebody had to." She gave him a tight, surprisingly tired smile. Then she pushed past him, shoving all her weight behind it. It took a lot for a human to make a chimera move.

He let her go, following her out into the snowy street. "Come on! I want to apologize."

She shot him a loathsome look over her shoulder. "No, you don't. You want to make yourself feel better."

He held back a frown as he weaved around Christmas shoppers. He really *did* want to apologize. She obviously hated his guts, and he couldn't have that. And more than that, she clearly had a lot of unresolved issues around this. She wouldn't be so angry if she didn't. She'd been getting better with her anger before he left, he'd assumed she kept it going. Seeing her beyond thirty and still snapping at people who didn't deserve it was... disconcerting. That employee back at the cafe, Hazel, had seemed genuinely scared of her. There was no way Emma wanted that.

"I really do want to apologize," he called after her. "Our last talk didn't go how I wanted it to."

Emma walked into the street, almost getting side-swiped by a car.

Arthur jogged after her, shooting the driver an apologetic wave.

She stopped just before the sidewalk, Cozy Grotto Cafe right in front of her. He could see Rusty through the window talking to one of the camera crew. The lighting rig was set up, the extras were being directed to their seats, and a makeup artist was fixing his costar's hair as she leaned on the counter, tapping away at her phone.

He knew he should go in. But all he could focus on was Emma, who turned to him with murder in her eyes.

"Oh, *didn't* it?" she spat. "You mean the talk where you *left* me on *Christmas Eve*? I had to go back to my parents and tell them why I was crying! You ruined Christmas!"

Arthur's traitorous heart twisted in his chest. He *hated* that he'd made her cry. She cried so rarely. He'd been shocked to see the first tear roll down her cheek as she yelled at him. Calling him a coward, a liar; vowing she'd never talk to him again.

"I invited you," he said, shocked at how much effort it took to keep his voice even. "*You're* the one who said no. You could've come."

She laughed up at him. "I was never going to come to LA! I'm not a city girl—I'm a Claw Haven girl. This is where I belong! And I'm super fucking happy! I wake up every day ecstatic that I didn't follow you to that vapid, empty, *pointless* city!"

"I'm happy it worked out for you," he repeated, clenching his teeth to keep the smile up. He should've realized she would test him. Nobody pushed his buttons like Emma, even after all these years. Fortunately, he was a good actor. Maybe it had been so long that even the legendary Emma Curt wouldn't be able to see through him.

Emma made a frustrated noise. "Ugh! I can't look at you, you're too annoying. *Don't* fuck up my cafe."

She stalked off down the street, shoppers parting as they noticed her fiery gaze.

He watched her go, marveling at the least successful interaction he'd had in the last decade. He used to watch her in class and wonder how such a small human could contain so much rage. What were the odds that she still did the same things to de-stress?

He cupped his hands over his mouth. "Go easy on the Cool Whip!"

She whirled on him, glaring. He allowed himself a smug grin. He so rarely got the last word with her. Then she opened her mouth, and he remembered there was a reason he didn't.

"Your sunglasses are stupid," she called back. "You look like a spoiled, out-of-touch jackass!"

Then she turned around and kept walking. Arthur let her, hoping none of the people looking his way were interested in giving a news outlet a quote. He'd worked hard on his public image. Getting into a screaming match with an old flame would be his first speck of dirt on an otherwise spotless record.

He ducked into the cafe, shaking snow off his wings.

Rusty rushed up, brushing the last flakes out of his mane. "Hey! Where'd you go?"

"Nowhere important." Arthur was annoyed to see his tail flicking, narrowly avoiding hitting a PA who was carrying a tray of coffee. He stilled it, smiling wider. "Are we ready?"

"Yeah, just setting up—"

Arthur cut him off with a gasp. There was a familiar face over near the far tables: a minotaur was sprucing up a vase of flowers and looking decidedly uncomfortable.

"Joshua Haberdash," he crowed, swerving around Rusty toward the minotaur, who jumped at the sound of his name. He looked surprised to see Arthur heading his way, his snout twisting up in a baffled smile as Arthur clapped him on the shoulder.

"You're a sight for sore eyes," he said, trying to ignore the uncomfortable feelings Emma had given him. Joshua was always good for a mood boost.

"Look at you!" he continued. "You finally hit your growth spurt!"

"Ha. Yeah, sure." Joshua gave him another nervous grin. "Growth spurt" was a joke; Joshua had always been huge, though he tried to hide it by hunching into his shoulders. He still had that annoying patch of fur hanging over his eyes, constantly getting brushed back behind his horns.

"You look great," Arthur said, relieved for an easy interaction. Joshua was always easy to talk to, happy to let Arthur chatter on while he nodded. Very agreeable guy. He even let Arthur copy his homework a few times.

"Thanks," Joshua said. "So do you, man. Um, I think your director wants to talk to you."

"He always does," Arthur said. He gave Joshua another shoulder clap. "Good to see you, bud! Hope you enjoy your little glimpse into the movie world."

"It's pretty fun," Joshua said again. "I'm just the flower guy."

"And you're doing great." Arthur shot him a thumbs-up and headed back over to Rusty, who was standing there with his hands on his hips, watching Arthur with that look that meant he wanted everything to happen much faster. But he still pulled up a tense smile, giving Arthur a questioning thumbs-up.

"You good?"

"I'm fantastic." Arthur shook his mane out, trying to hold onto the brief boost that seeing Joshua had given him. He hadn't expected to be happy to see anybody in town, so Joshua had been a nice surprise. But the uncomfortable feelings were creeping back, unwanted and unearned. She couldn't get mad at him for something that happened when they were *teenagers*. They were over thirty now. It was ancient history.

Rusty snapped his fingers in front of his muzzle. "Hey! Movie star!"

"I'm here," Arthur said. "Where do you want me?"

Rusty gave him a dubious look, but pointed at his mark—right in front of Jennifer Hertzman, who waved enthusiastically.

"Hey," she said, batting her makeup guy away and pulling Arthur into a careful hug. "How are you? This place is a winter wonderland—you never said!"

"It was less of a wonderland when I lived here," he admitted, accepting her hug gratefully. Jennifer was fun and uncomplicated, everything he liked in a girl. Everything he liked in a *person*, period.

"Don't let the PR team hear you say that," she laughed as she pulled back. "I overheard the extras whispering."

Arthur's ear twitched. "Oh?"

She giggled, thankfully not noticing his unease. "Yeah! Everyone's *so* excited you're back. I bet you're *pumped*."

"You bet." He flashed his fangs and let the makeup guy come at him with a comb, straightening his whiskers. He hadn't even noticed they were crooked. The makeup guy took the sunglasses next, and Arthur tried not to think about what Emma had told him. They weren't *dumb*. Rusty had assured him he made them work.

Rusty raised a megaphone. "Alright! Everybody, positions!"

Arthur rolled his shoulders, watching everyone get into place. He couldn't quite remember which scene they were doing. His mind kept drifting back to the raw fury in Emma's eyes as she hissed at him on the street. She always told him to stop hiding everything under a smile, but she hid too. She just hid behind her anger. In Arthur's opinion, his was the better tactic. Everybody wanted to be smiled at. Nobody wanted to be screamed at.

"Hey," he whispered as Rusty made one last adjustment with the lighting crew. "Were my sunglasses stupid?"

She blinked, pausing the pre-scene jumps she always did before a take. "What?"

"The sunglasses I was wearing before," he explained. "I could pull them off, right?"

She laughed. "Of course! You're Arthur Pineclaw. You can pull off anything."

It was just what he needed to hear. He winked at her, his lines flowing back into his head as easy as flipping a switch. They were doing the meeting scene, the two lovers from the big city running into each other in a middle-of-nowhere town. His character was confident, aloof, and charming—his favorite kind of character to play. He did it every day, after all.

"Alright," Rusty called. "And... action!"

FOUR

Emma had been hoping for outrage. For her mom to gasp and her dad to swear vengeance.

She was *not* expecting her mom to lean closer to the screen and ask if she could get an autograph.

"Mom," Emma said, scandalized. "I'm *not* asking him for an autograph!"

"I'm just saying," Bitsey Curt said from the phone screen, adjusting her floppy sun hat. "He was in that *In Too Deep* movie! You know, the one with that mermaid we love! What was her name, honey?"

"Penelope Cruise," Glen Curt replied. "And she's *kidding*, hon. Of course, your mother doesn't want an autograph. We liked him—"

"I know," Emma said icily.

"And *In Too Deep* was great, but that damn chimera broke your heart," Glen finished.

"He didn't *break* it," Emma argued. She stretched her shirt over her knees, pulling her comforter further up.

She had to get dressed soon, and she was still psyching herself up to head out into the cold. The snow had stopped, but it was even colder than yesterday. Just because Emma was used to this cold didn't mean she liked it.

Her parents looked at each other knowingly. Emma didn't know why she bothered to lie: they'd been right there picking up the pieces. Feeding her soup and putting up with her yelling at romantic movies. The breakup had affected her an embarrassing amount. She should've been able to get on with life. Instead, she'd halved her hours at the supermarket and moved back in with her parents.

Emma sighed. "How's the cruise going?"

"It's warm," Bitsey replied, as she always did. They'd started on the cruise just as Claw Haven tipped into winter. Bitsey loved pointing out how warm she was, and at *Christmas*, no less. Emma tried not to take it personally. She would hate being on a cruise—there was nowhere to escape when she needed to clear her head. All those quiz nights and games and annoying sunbathers. But for the first time, she was annoyed that she had turned down her parents' offer to go on the cruise with them. They got back in the New Year. She could've avoided Arthur entirely.

Bitsey continued, "Are you sure you don't want us to cut the trip short? We're docking soon; we could get a flight back."

"No," Emma replied instantly. "It's fine."

Her parents traded another look.

"It's just," her dad started. "When we decided to

leave you alone at Christmas, we didn't think you'd be stuck with the guy who broke your heart for weeks on end."

"Only two weeks! And I'm not *alone at Christmas*. I have, like, eight different invites to people's houses. And I don't even need to *see* him if I don't want to. I could just let the others take care of the cafe—"

"Which you won't," Glen said. "You're going to be there every day, just in case someone tries to put something in your fridges again."

"You don't need to worry," Emma said over him. "I'm totally fine. Honestly, I couldn't care less that he's around. He's nothing to me."

Bitsey hummed, pushing her floppy sun hat out of her eyes again. "Isn't that his shirt?"

Emma glared down at her sleep shirt. *Shit*. This *was* the shirt she'd stolen off of him in junior year. It was so faded and worn she'd forgotten about its origins. She would've thrown it out with everything else if she'd found it earlier, but she'd only rediscovered it a few years ago when she was sifting through her parents' garage for a yard sale.

"No," Emma insisted. "Of course not."

"Of course not," Glen echocd, looking like he didn't buy it in the slightest. Then he sighed. "You're talking to people, right? You're not holing up in your room and yelling at romantic movies?"

"No," Emma said, pushing her DVDs out of view. "I'm talking, Dad. Don't worry about me."

Her parents traded yet another look.

"Daisy said you were particularly snappy the other day," Glen said. "You only get like that when you're upset, hon. I thought you were trying to be nicer to that new human."

"I'm not upset! And Daisy needs to quit texting you. It's weird!" Emma rolled her eyes. "I have to get to the cafe. Shooting starts soon, and I wasn't there yesterday."

"They might've burned the place down," Bitsey agreed.

"Bye," Emma said flatly.

She waved at her sunscreen-sticky parents and ended the call. Then she sat back, growling with annoyance. Her parents needed to stay out of her business. Daisy, too, that little backstabber. Who cared if she was snappy? Hazel needed to quit pissing her off. *Everybody* did. If people stopped being so annoying, she wouldn't have to yell at them.

She got up and paused, plucking at her traitorous sleep shirt. It didn't *mean* anything. It was just really, really comfortable.

It didn't stop her from throwing the offending garment in the trash after she got out of the shower.

The cafe was full of lights, the camera crew, and local extras, who were all way too excited to be on a movie set. Most of them avoided Emma's eyes as she came in, the bolder ones sending her a sympathetic glance.

Emma forced herself not to glare at them. They meant well. They didn't know that getting sympathy felt like getting a slap to the face. Emma didn't want *sympathy*. There was nothing to be sympathetic *about*. She was fine! Who cared if her ex was back in town? It didn't affect her. And if her breath caught as she watched him swagger out of the backrooms with a makeup guy following behind and brushing out his mane, it was totally unrelated.

Daisy sidled up beside her, looping a furry arm under Emma's. "I won't ask how you're doing."

"Good," Emma said. "If you did, I'd fire you. Quit texting my parents."

"*They* texted *me*," Daisy protested with a smile.

Emma sighed. Daisy was bright and bubbly and incredibly efficient, the perfect worker to offset Hazel's well-meaning ditziness. Plus all the customers loved her — she was always there with an agreeable smile, ready to get you whatever you needed. Even if that was a listening ear. Some locals came in just to talk to Daisy, who was all too happy to listen. It was her one flaw—sometimes she got too tied up in chatting to concentrate on the growing line.

"But I'm here if you need to talk," Daisy continued, her ears flattening in dreaded sympathy. "About anything."

"Do me a favor and shut up." Emma pulled at her apron. "Wait, no. I want to talk about these stupid uniforms they gave you. What's wrong with ours?"

"Not movie-looking enough, I guess." Daisy did a little spin, apron swishing out around her.

Hazel appeared on the other side of her, waving excitedly. "Boss! Hey! Sorry you couldn't stick around yesterday; it was super fun. We just did the same stuff over and over for every scene. It got really relaxing. You sure you don't want to try it? I'm sure they'd let you!"

Emma gritted her teeth, trying not to think about what her parents had said this morning. She *was* being nicer to Hazel. When Hazel deserved it, anyway.

"I'm fine," Emma replied, then clamped her mouth shut. She could see Arthur out of the corner of her eye, leaning on the counter to talk to that damn director who told Luna to keep his star's identity a secret. If he'd let her, they could've avoided the whole mess. He'd be at some other Claw Haven cafe, and Emma would be able to ignore him properly.

"I hope you and Arthur get to catch up today," Hazel continued, twisting her apron nervously. "He said you guys didn't get much of a chance yesterday."

Emma stared at her. "He said what?"

Daisy cut in. "He just mentioned that you two talked."

"And that he wanted to keep the conversation going," Hazel added. Then she winced. Daisy had just dug an elbow into her side. "Ow! What? He did say that! And he seems really nice. I don't see why the boss is so against it."

"He's not *nice*," Emma said flatly. "He's a self-centered jackass who only cares about his next close-up and having someone around to buff his claws. Don't let him trick you just because his mane is shiny."

"It *is* very shiny," Hazel said. "And soft."

Emma felt a ridiculous stab of jealousy at the implication, followed by an even bigger stab of frustration. Why should she care if Arthur was letting impressionable young extras touch his mane?

Arthur's carefully trimmed ears twitched. He turned away from Rusty to look at Emma, face splitting into an infuriatingly smug grin.

Emma very maturely resisted the urge to flip him off.

"I'm going to do some office work," she said darkly. "Don't let them touch anything important."

"On it," Daisy said.

Emma paused and turned to Hazel. "And don't fall for the mane trick again. It's Chimera Flirting 101. Don't do it again. He is *not* worth it."

Hazel's eyes widened. "Oh! Oh...kay?"

She looked genuinely shocked. Like she hadn't picked up on being flirted with at all.

Emma swallowed a sour taste in her mouth. "You know what? Do whatever you want. Touch his mane all over. Touch his wings while you're at it, he likes that."

"Um," Hazel said.

Emma didn't stick around to hear her reply. She stalked into the backrooms, away from the extras shooting her awkward looks and Daisy trying to find something to say and a strange pressure she was sure was Arthur's gaze on the back of her head.

But when she turned back to glance through the door that led to the backrooms, Arthur was looking at Rusty again. Nodding and laughing, his eyes creasing so beautifully it made Emma's breath catch.

The door swung shut.

Emma squeezed her eyes shut, forcing the warm coil in her stomach to go away. She just hadn't gotten any in a while. That was the problem. If she'd been *satisfied* recently, she wouldn't have any reaction to his stupid, sexy face at all, ex-boyfriend or otherwise.

It was better this way, Emma told herself as she pored over the paperwork. She'd been meaning to sort out this tax stuff for months. Now she finally had a chance: she could lock herself in the office, and nobody would be knocking on the door asking where they kept the receipt rolls or how to void a sale without restarting their glitchy POS systems.

A knock on the door jolted her out of her annoyed paperwork haze.

She sighed, scooting her wheely chair over and grabbing the door. "What?"

Rusty blinked down at her. He had on a backwards cap with a pen shoved behind his ear, his glasses magnifying his eyes to double the size.

"Hey," he said distractedly. "Want to be an extra?"

Emma glared. "I can't think of something I'd rather do less. Bye."

She started to close the door.

Rusty shoved his foot in the way. "We need someone who can carry four plates at once."

"So get Daisy."

"She burned her hand."

"What?" Emma stopped trying to pull the door closed on his foot. "How?"

Rusty sighed. "As I understand it, your other employee—"

"*Goddamnit*, Hazel. Is Daisy okay?"

"She'll be back tomorrow."

Emma looked longingly at the paperwork she'd just been stressing over. "How long would this last? I'm busy."

"Just a few takes."

She eyed him. Rusty had been all smiles when he met her yesterday, but they were all perfunctory. Fleeting. He had completely ignored anyone unless he thought they were important. Exactly the kind of LA bullshit Emma had expected out of him.

He examined his watch. "We're kind of on a schedule. So either you come with me, or I start scouting the other cafes, and I'd really rather—"

"I get paid as an extra on top of my usual renting rates?"

He shrugged. "Sure."

Emma stood, her wheely chair bouncing off her desk. "Let's get this over with."

She held still for the makeup artist. She even put up with one of the assistants fixing her collar, getting up in her personal space without asking. But she drew the line at *giggling*.

"It's just a little giggle," Rusty said, a look on his face

like he regretted not grabbing someone from Creature Comforts. "You go over, he says the line, and then you—"

"Giggle, no, I heard you." Emma glared over at Arthur, who was currently sitting at a window table with his costar seated opposite him. They were talking idly between takes, the costar reaching over to bat his shoulder. *She* was a giggler. She looked adorable, nose scrunching up like a chipmunk, head tipping back. The kind of girl who put up with Arthur's bullshit. She was probably charmed by it. Just like the girl that Rusty was telling Emma to be.

"I'm not an actor," she reminded Rusty. "You said I'd just be standing there."

"Script rewrites." Rusty rubbed his cap tiredly. "Fine. No giggle. Just... have *some* reaction. Alright? Some realistic reaction that shows how much his flirting affects you."

Emma stared at the back of Arthur's head. Did he put his director up to this? Would he really go that far? She wouldn't put it past him to try something like this. But it seemed... cruel. He was never *cruel*—not on purpose, anyway. Just careless.

"I thought he was romancing blondie," she said.

"He is. He's showing her how seductive he can be."

Emma laughed bitterly. "Sure. And why am I carrying all the plates?"

"It shows how busy you are. Which makes it all the more effective when he makes you pause."

Emma regretted ever giving Luna Musgrove the time of day.

An assistant handed her the plates of cold food. Emma stacked three along one arm, then took the cold coffee with her free hand.

"Alright," Rusty called over the still cafe. "Everybody in place? Great. Action!"

Arthur and his costar started talking, leaning over the table like something was pulling them together. Even fuming, Emma had to give it to him: he played his role well. Hollywood had typecast him as the handsome, charismatic chimera who could either save the day or reveal he was the bad guy at the end of the movie. But he was always smooth, no matter what. Always dazzling and confident.

That was what Emma had heard, anyway. She hadn't watched any of his movies.

Rusty nudged her. "Your cue," he whispered.

Emma blinked. She hadn't been listening for the line.

She walked toward the table. *Act like you usually would during the lunch rush,* Rusty had told her. *You're expecting a normal interaction, in and out.*

Emma slid the plates onto the table. They were leaning toward each other so far that it was hard to put the plates down.

"I can prove it," Arthur was telling his costar. Then he turned toward Emma. "Thanks for—"

He stopped, startled. Maybe he *hadn't* put Rusty up to this, Emma realized.

"Cut," Rusty yelled. "Arthur, what was that?"

Arthur straightened, pulling up that megawatt smile once more. "Sorry, Rust. I didn't know you were bringing old friends on board! Is Daisy okay?"

"She'll be back tomorrow. We made do," Rusty said, flipping distractedly through a clipboard. "Let's reset."

Emma walked back out of the frame, hoping her cheeks didn't look as hot as they felt. She could see Hazel giving her a thumbs-up from behind the counter, which she resolutely ignored. She was worried that Hazel would try to apologize for burning Daisy again if she made eye contact, and Emma would snap at her again.

"Okay," Rusty declared. "And... action!"

Arthur and his costar sunk back into the conversation. This time Emma actually listened to their lines. They were talking about their exes and what attracted them to them in the first place. Arthur was arguing that seduction was about playing a part. Showing them what they want to see.

"There's an art to it," he said.

That was Emma's cue. She strode out, clenching the plates so her hands wouldn't shake. She hated how much of an effect his stupid monologue was having on her. She'd been over their relationship in her head so many times since he left—*was* it all an act? Did he ever really love her, or was she just something to entertain him before he escaped to bigger horizons?

"I can prove it," Arthur continued. This time when he looked up at Emma, his dazzling smile didn't falter.

"Thanks for that," he told her as she set the food down.

Emma didn't respond. She sometimes didn't when it got this busy, just shooting them a distracted smile and then shooting off to whatever needed doing next. *You don't need to giggle*, she told herself as she slid the cold coffee in front of him. *Just need to look up at him and—*

Arthur's warm fingers brushed her chin.

Emma looked up, hand tightening around the coffee cup. Suddenly she was seventeen again, sitting under the bleachers after gym class. Watching him tip her head back with those big, gentle fingers. Saying—

"Hey, beautiful. I hope that coffee's as sweet as you."

Emma blinked, coming back to the present. His fingers were still on her chin. Thumb and forefinger, just like he used to. For a moment his eyes were so soft she could almost fool herself into thinking time had folded in on itself and they were back under the bleachers again that very first time.

Then he smiled. It was a movie star smile, the one she used to catch him practicing in the mirror.

White hot rage blossomed all over her body. How dare he pull this crap on her? Showing up at her cafe, following her when she tried to storm off. And now he was touching her just like he used to, grinning like it was a *joke*.

She could feel the director's eyes on her, waiting.

You want a reaction? Emma thought. *I'll give you a reaction.*

She turned the cup over, sending a torrent of coffee into Arthur's lap.

FIVE

"Look on the bright side," Jennifer told him as he came out of the backrooms in fresh clothes. "She could've got you with *hot* coffee."

Arthur forced a laugh. He very badly wanted it to be a real laugh, but no matter how hard he tried to talk himself into it while he was getting changed, he couldn't find the situation funny. Which was odd. It was a good anecdote. Something to bring up at parties when they'd talk about crazy exes. But Arthur just kept thinking back to Emma's outrage. More than that, she'd looked *betrayed*. Maybe he'd gone too far with the chin-touch. It was one thing to flirt with her for a scene, it was entirely another to improvise his old move. He couldn't help it—it felt so natural. Like he was seventeen again, teasing her between classes. Trying to make that scowl slip into a smile.

Sometimes it worked. Other times, it backfired horribly. He'd been so eager to get a reaction out of her he'd forgotten how badly it could go.

"So," Jennifer said, sipping coffee through a straw so she didn't mess up her lipstick. "*Bad* breakup, huh?"

"It happened a long time ago. But yeah, I guess you could say that." Arthur straightened his collar, scanning the crowded cafe. Emma was standing in the corner, looking murderous as Rusty bent close to whisper-yell at her.

Arthur grimaced. Somebody had to get in the middle of that before somebody lost an eye.

"—completely unacceptable," Rusty was saying as Arthur squeezed around the cafe tables toward them. "I don't care if he danced with some other girl at prom or didn't put your photo up in his locker, alright? This is a multi-million-dollar production, and Luna said you were a *professional*—"

Emma opened her mouth, ready to tear into him.

Arthur pulled up a grin and slid into place next to Rusty. "Rust! I'm pretty again, are you ready to go?"

Rusty tried to rearrange his pissed-off expression into the usual encouraging look Arthur was used to. He didn't do a great job. There was a reason he was a director, not an actor.

"Arthur, buddy." Rusty pinched the bridge of his nose. "Just give me one second. I'm wrapping things up here."

"I can see that," Arthur said smoothly. "Mind if I cut in? I wanted to apologize. I got caught up in the scene and forgot it wasn't a good idea to grab extras when they're holding coffee. Hope you're not too mad at her for a spill, Rust. Could've happened to anyone."

They stared at him. Arthur kept smiling. There was no way they bought this—Emma had obviously done it on purpose. But he could see them processing: he'd given them an out. They just had to take it.

"I had an extra who dropped a cream cheese bagel on my face during a monologue," Arthur said to Emma. "This is small potatoes. I had a beard back then; they had to scrub it out! This time I just had to change my clothes. No harm done. Right, Rust?"

"Right," Rusty said slowly. He tugged his cap down harder, a nervous tic he usually only did after at least ten hours on set, and looked back at Emma. "Back to makeup. We're almost finished with the reset."

Emma shot Arthur a curious look. He smiled wider, hope flaring in his chest. It was the least hostile look she'd given him since he arrived back in Claw Haven. He counted that as progress.

Rusty waited for her to get out of earshot before he leaned in. "Whatever you guys have going on—"

"Had," Arthur corrected.

"Whatever. Make sure this doesn't happen again, alright?"

"Of course! Hey…" Arthur bent closer, lowering his voice and hoping that there weren't any werewolves or vampires listening in from across the room. Super-hearing monsters usually tried not to eavesdrop, but he was famous. He wouldn't blame them for wanting movie star drama.

"It was a good move, right? Like, it worked. For the scene."

Rusty hesitated. For a moment, Arthur thought he might've actually fucked up.

"It worked," Rusty said. "You're doing great, man. Your ex is just crazy."

Arthur fought down an involuntary wave of annoyance at hearing someone call Emma crazy. He had the strangest urge to tell Rusty to shut his face. Rusty didn't *know* Emma. He didn't get to call her anything.

"Right," Arthur said. "Great. I'll just..."

He hooked a thumb behind him at his mark. Rusty nodded, waving him over. Arthur made his way between the tables to the table where Jennifer was already sitting, her hair perfect and her makeup untouched.

Arthur sat down, relieved to sink back into character. It was one of his favorite things about acting: everything else fell away. He didn't have to worry about anything but the script in front of him.

"Ready," Rusty called. "And... action!"

Arthur started in on his lines. Jennifer tossed hers back. They bounced off each other easily, the chemistry they'd discovered in the screen test blooming to life just like it did with everyone Arthur got paired with.

"There's an art to it," Arthur said, trying not to seem too aware of the woman who was heading toward them. "I can prove it."

He looked at Emma. She was sliding plates of food onto the table, not meeting their eyes. She looked distracted, just like she was directed to.

Arthur leaned into her space. He meant to say it cool and confident like last time. But something changed as the words made their way up his throat.

"Hey, beautiful. I hope that coffee's as sweet as you."

Emma froze. On the other side of the table, Jennifer's brows rose almost imperceptibly.

Shit, Arthur thought. That was *not* the tone he'd been aiming for. Those words had come out so soft and sweet he was shocked to hear it come from him. That wasn't his Flirting With A Waitress voice. That was his Love Confession Scene voice—humbled and stripped bare. The voice he didn't bring out until the last third of the movie. Where the hell had that come from?

Arthur was about to sit up and call for another try. But Emma was still staring at him. There was no rage in her face this time. Instead, she looked... flustered. Her cheeks went red and her eyelids fluttered prettily. Then she jerked up and turned away, walking off toward the camera crew.

"And cut," Rusty called. "Okay! That's a wrap on that scene. Let's move on."

Emma pushed through the crew and disappeared into the backrooms.

Arthur watched her go, heart in his throat. He had the sinking feeling he'd just fucked up—*properly* fucked up, no excuses to make it better. No matter how much Rusty or Jennifer would tell him she was being crazy, it didn't matter. He wouldn't feel better until she absolved him.

Jennifer giggled across from him. "Wow. She was

actually pretty good. Why didn't you do that the first time?"

Arthur laughed woodenly, still watching the doors. She was leaving, he was sure of it. He had to catch her.

"Okay," Rusty continued. "Let's keep going from that last line."

Arthur stood, hardly aware he was doing it. "Two minutes! I need to use the bathroom."

Annoyance flickered over Rusty's face, then it was gone.

"Two minutes," he said.

Emma was pulling on her handbag when he found her.

"Hey," he said from her office doorway. "Can we talk?"

"Nope. Tell the director I'm not in any more scenes." She jerked her head for him to move. "Come on, get out of the doorway."

His hands flexed against the flimsy wood, shocked to hear it creak. He let go of it fast. It had been a while since he'd misjudged his own strength. It'd happened so often with Emma that he'd forgotten.

"I just wanted you to know I'm suing you," he tried. "You damaged some priceless equipment with that little stunt back there."

No dice. He tensed, waiting for another knotty barb. But it didn't come. She just glared at him, shoulders up near her ears.

"Just get out of the way," she hissed. "I *will* scream."

He didn't doubt it. He moved out of the way, barely resisting the urge to reach out and grab her shoulder. She was heading for the door, ready to walk back into the cafe and past all those people. If he didn't say it now, he was never going to say it.

"I shouldn't have touched you," he said in a rush.

Emma stopped.

"It was out of line. I was thinking about what would be good for the scene, not for—" Arthur swallowed, uncharacteristically nervous. "I didn't think. I'm sorry."

He smiled harder, sweat pricking his fur. He hadn't genuinely apologized for a long time. It was always empty platitudes, whatever he had to say to make things right. No guilt, no mess, everybody came out of it happy. He wasn't used to this churning in his gut. He thought he'd escaped it with Claw Haven.

Emma turned. Her handbag dangled near her hip. It was very similar to the one she'd worn in the last year he'd known her. Maybe it even was. The leather sure *looked* a decade old.

"You actually sounded like you believed that," she told him.

"I do," Arthur said, surprised. Now he was thinking about it, blindsiding his ex with a romantic touch during a movie scene she didn't want to be in *did* sound like a pretty stupid move.

"Look," he tried. "I want to make things right. If you're going to be hanging around set, we can't have you throwing coffee in my face—"

"I didn't throw anything at your face," she said icily. "Yet."

"Much appreciated." Arthur tried another grin. It fell flat in a way that his smiles rarely did anymore. He thought he'd gotten them down to an art. He *had* gotten them down to an art. Except when Emma Curt was around, apparently.

"We don't have to be friends," he continued. "We just have to play nice. Let me take you to dinner; we'll find some way to have a civil conversation."

She narrowed her eyes. It used to drive him crazy when she did that. It meant she was scrutinizing him, sizing him up. So many people got flustered or giddy, too busy falling over his charm to look past it. But not Emma.

"Why," she began slowly, "would I let you do that?"

A strand of hair fell out of her pixie cut, hanging over her eyes. Arthur itched with a shockingly powerful urge to brush it out of her face. He clenched his hand. He'd just experienced the consequences of touching her once. He didn't want to do it again before he'd won her over.

"I know you like being angry," he said. "It's relaxing for you. But *this*..."

He made a coffee-throwing gesture toward his lap. Which, watching her face crease up, could understandably be taken as another gesture entirely.

"This isn't the kind of anger you like," he continued. "You like being *annoyed*. You don't like this... volcanic crap."

"Yeah, well. It comes with having you around."

He decided not to be hurt by that. He pulled his shoulders back, realizing they'd been slinking inward during this conversation.

"Let me fix it," he offered. "I promise by tomorrow night, you'll want to murder me a little less."

Her eyes narrowed even further. Her mouth opened, and his heart sank as he realized what her reply was going to be. He wanted her to say yes. He needed her to say yes. He *needed* to fix this; he needed it with a narrowmindedness that he hadn't felt in a long time.

"Please," he said, letting some genuine desperation creep into his voice. She always liked it when he made himself small for her.

Half my size and you can still undo me, he'd told her. She'd liked to quote it back to him, once upon a time. Nobody had undone him like that since. It was a relief. Relationships were easier when they didn't make you talk about difficult crap. Especially *your* difficult crap. And yet some part of him, a strange, murky part he didn't let himself look at very often, missed it. The aftermath, anyway. He had never known himself better than when he was with her—had never felt so close to another person. His relationships before and since had always been committed to having a good time and not much else. No digging, no calling each other out. Just easy fun until it inevitably fizzled out.

Emma sighed, dragging him back to the present.

"You're paying," she told him.

. . .

Arthur rode that high all the way back to the Musgrove Inn after filming shut down for the day.

The lobby was full. A mer looked bored in the corner, and an orc bent down to fix her wheelchair. A gargoyle grabbed his scarf from a coat rack with a scowl.

At the end of it sat a long reception desk. The human receptionist stared down at her phone and giggled, twisting her frizzy red hair around her fingers. She laughed again as Arthur approached, so loud and high-pitched that Arthur flinched. Sensitive ears.

"Excuse me," he started. "Is Luna Musgrove around?"

The receptionist looked up, startled. "Oh! Hiya! Yes, I think she's—"

Before she could continue, Luna emerged from the backroom. Her hand was locked in a broad man's shirt, pulling him out into the lobby with a playful grin. The man was watching her with eyes so dark Arthur almost felt he was intruding. He was obviously the husband— even if he didn't stink of an alpha werewolf, him bending in to nuzzle her neck was proof enough.

The receptionist waved. "Luna! This gentleman's looking for you."

"Thanks, Jaz," Luna said, scratching her husband's scalp before pulling him back. Her eyebrows shot up as she noticed Arthur standing at the counter. "Arthur! What are you doing here? Oh, this is my husband, Oliver. Ollie, tell him about that movie you liked."

Oliver shot her a wry look and held out a hand

towards Arthur. "Good to meet you. I liked your spy character in *Mane Suspect.*"

"That was a fun one," Arthur said cheerily, pumping his hand. "Thanks for getting the inn back up and working again. Bet you guys get more business than the last owners."

He gestured behind them at the lobby. He'd never actually set foot in the inn when he was growing up, but he'd seen it looking sad and decrepit on Cliff Street as he walked to school. He'd be surprised if they got even a third of their rooms filled at any one time.

"Thanks to Luna," Oliver agreed. They looked at each other softly, and Arthur was given the repeated impression that he was intruding.

Then Luna tore her gaze away, blinking rapidly. "Right! What can I do for you? Is there something wrong with the cabin?"

"The cabin's fine. I was wondering if you could help me out with something." He leaned over the desk. "I'm looking to take a girl out to dinner. But she's a local, so she already knows every place in town. Any suggestions?"

Luna smirked. "I got you covered."

Six

"Well," Emma said as she opened the door the following night. "At least you're not wearing sunglasses."

Arthur beamed at her. He was dressed in a sleek gray suit, the collar unbuttoned to show off the thin fur over his stupidly defined collarbones.

She herded him out onto the ramp, closing the door behind her. "Where are we going?"

"Can't tell you all my secrets yet." He reached to place a hand around her waist. She elbowed him away with a scowl and headed toward the street.

"This isn't a date," she reminded him, heart pounding from his proximity. "This is dinner. Where you promised to make me want to murder you less. I'm still feeling murdery."

"Give it time," he said.

She pushed the gate open and frowned. She couldn't see any unfamiliar cars parked on the snowy street. She'd half been hoping that he'd brought the limo so she could make fun of it.

He followed her, wings flexing. "I *do* need to touch you for this next part."

"Oh, do you? What, are you lifting me gallantly over a puddle? Newsflash, everything is frozen. So keep your paws—" She cut off with a yelp as he scooped her into his arms, wings flaring out.

He grinned down at her. "Hold on."

Then he took off. Flying higher and higher, clearing the rooftops. Emma gasped as cold air stung her face. Whenever he took her flying in the old days, she'd bury her face in his mane to keep out the chill. Like hell she was going to do that now.

"How are you doing?" he asked.

She spat out a strand of golden mane.

"Go fuck yourself," she managed. But it came out far too close to a laugh.

His grin widened. He held her tighter, wings sturdy and powerful as he flew them toward the mountains. She stared up at them as they worked. She'd assumed that his wings would be frail and useless after so long in LA with everyone driving him around. She should've known he would take his wing workouts seriously; not even a life of luxury would stop him from going flying in the mornings.

She didn't dare glance down. She'd learned her lesson in high school after looking down during a romantic Valentine's Day fly and nearly throttling him as she realized she *was*, in fact, afraid of heights. A fact that he laughed heartily at when they got back to the ground.

You had nothing to worry about, he'd told her. *I have you.*

She tightened her grip, forcing the unwelcome memory out. He didn't *have* her. Not anymore. He just... wasn't letting her fall. These old emotions had no right to come crawling back, some long-lost echo of how she used to feel in his arms, warm and comforted and *safe* even at the highest heights.

He landed halfway up the mountain, his shoes sinking into the snow. "Here we are."

Emma twisted. He was taking her toward a fancy log cabin.

"There's no *way* that was the only way up," she protested, squirming out of his arms.

"There's a path," he agreed. "This was faster."

"Oh, faster. Sure." She grimaced at her boots. They were too short, snow leaking through her jeans. She had assumed she'd be dealing with the ankle-length snow around town, which had been cleared entirely around the main streets. She hadn't been expecting to go up on a *mountain*.

He pulled the sliding glass door open. "After you."

She glowered at him and stepped inside, shaking her boots off as messily as she could.

He stepped in after her, giving her an appreciative look. "You look nice."

"I do not," she retorted, heading down the hall. She hadn't even done her hair, her pixie cut sticking out even crazier than usual thanks to the unexpected flying trip up the mountain. "You look like a jackass."

He followed her, tugging at his collar. "I'm not even wearing a tie!"

"It's your face. Where's dinner? My lunch was..." She stopped.

The living room was irritatingly gorgeous. Lush, dark carpet and plants hanging from the ceiling. A fireplace smoldered in the corner. But that wasn't what drew her eye: it was the view. The rear wall was made of glass, and the town of Claw Haven splayed out underneath them.

"Beautiful," Arthur said.

She jumped. He was closer than she thought. She spun around to see him lingering behind her, looking out at the tiny, glittering town with a strange look in his eyes. Almost like longing. Then he blinked, and the look was replaced by his loathsome charm as he looked down at her.

"Best seat in the house," he informed her. "Luna set it up for me. The cabin was set up last year, and I'm the first one to stay in it."

"Lucky you," Emma said dryly. But she couldn't keep a stubborn hint of awe out of her voice. She hadn't seen the town from up above since... shit. Since the last time that he flew her up the mountain. He used to take her up here sometimes in the summer for picnics. She'd never seen it in the dark before. It really was beautiful—a small, gleaming jewel in the darkness.

Arthur cleared his throat. "So! You were talking about dinner? It's in the kitchen."

She snorted, following him. "Oh god. Don't tell me you cooked."

"I wouldn't subject you to that," he said, mock-gravelly. "You know Heath? He owns the bakery now."

"You don't say."

"Yeah, and it turns out he isn't just good at baking."

"Yeah. He's also good at bitching." Emma's laugh was cut short when Arthur pulled a tray out of the oven: two steaming bowls of risotto, with a warm loaf cut into thick, fluffy slices.

"I hope you still like mushroom risotto," Arthur said, carrying the tray back toward the living room. "I told him to make it extra creamy."

There were peas dotted alongside the mushrooms. Emma wondered if he'd asked for that as well. Silky risotto with peas and mushrooms, a pat of butter melted in the middle—just the way she liked it.

Arthur paused at the doorway. "Are you coming?"

"What?" Emma swallowed around a mortifyingly thick throat. "Yeah. Coming."

She followed him back into the living room, sitting on her knees at the coffee table across from him. He kept talking as he pulled the oven mitts off and set up the cutlery, but Emma couldn't stop staring at the damn risotto, trying to stop her eyes from stinging. What the hell did he think he was doing? What was *she* doing agreeing to this?

Arthur ate a spoonful of risotto. "*Mm*. That's wonderful. Try some."

Emma picked up her spoon and considered throwing

it at his nose. She dunked it in the risotto instead, telling herself she could always leave. She'd threaten to walk down the mountain if she had to, and he'd give in and fly her down. She was pretty sure. He liked pissing her off, but he never wanted to *really* upset her. Not unless he had to, anyway. He hated it when people were mad at him—her especially. Apparently, that still mattered to him.

She took a grudging mouthful of risotto. It was warm and earthy and comforting, and she couldn't stop herself from letting out an appreciative hum.

"Right?" Arthur said. "Not as good as your mom makes it, but still pretty damn good."

He ate another spoonful. His tail flicked happily. He looked so *relaxed,* with his collar open and wings fanning out against the couch behind him. It made Emma think back to one of the first insults she'd ever paid him, back in freshman year. He'd been asking her why she was annoyed with him when everybody else in school loved him. She'd snapped back at him. She couldn't remember the exact words, but it was something like *you look like the kind of guy who takes "fake it til you make it" too seriously.*

He still did. Every genuine emotion got hastily covered up by a picture-perfect smile and a line tailored to suit whatever he thought people wanted to hear. There was nothing true there unless you yanked it back, exposing all those normal insecurities and a deep-seated belief that nobody would like him if he wasn't *on* all the time. Charming and charismatic and *dreamy* 24/7. Was all that still there? Or had he glued that switch down so it never turned off?

She dropped her spoon into her risotto with a clatter. "You can't impress me, you know."

Arthur made a questioning noise, his mouth full. There was a smudge of risotto on his furry chin, which Emma refused to find adorable.

"All this," she said, gesturing at the incredible view, the cabin, and the food. "I know who you are under all this crap."

Arthur's ears twitched. He swallowed his risotto, wiping his mouth neatly.

"And who am I?" he asked, shooting her a bright smile like this was an interview, not a tense chat between two exes.

For a second, Emma felt... *sad* for him. She wrestled it down as soon as it appeared, but she still felt it. She wondered if he let any of his other girlfriends hold him while he cried at the end of Mermaid and Me, or if he'd vented to them after a particularly empty phone call with his parents. If he ever told them about his recurring nightmare of walking through a crowd, shouting and waving his arms, but nobody ever saw him.

Maybe he did. But she fucking doubted it.

It didn't matter anyway. The chimera she'd fallen in love with was long gone. He'd left on Christmas Eve a million years ago, and he wasn't coming back. Even if he was sitting across from her, his gaze getting oddly desperate the longer she didn't reply.

Emma took a deep breath. "You're a self-seeking, fame-hungry jackass."

"Again with the jackass," Arthur said quietly and sighed. "Look—"

"I'm not finished," Emma barked. "You're that same asshole who walked away from your entire life to chase a dream. You *knew* I'd never come with you, and you did it anyway. It was more important because it involved *you*. You *always* come first. Nothing matters more to Arthur Pineclaw than Arthur Pineclaw."

"Emma—"

"You're that same guy who never wanted to talk about his feelings, or *anyone's* feelings, because feelings are hard and messy and you want things to be *easy*. Congratulations! You did it! Everything's easy for you now, Arthur. Including people. Everybody falling over themselves to please you, nobody ever digging deeper. Which is what you always wanted! How does it feel, movie star? Does it feel good? Forming a lot of long-lasting, deep connections in Hollywood? Or is everything all —all bright and breezy and no strings attached, let's not talk about anything *hard*, let's not try to see each other because that's so much *easier*."

She stopped, panting. Her eyes were burning again.

Arthur stared down at his risotto. She'd expected him to look surprised. And he did, for a moment. But only for a moment. His wings flexed behind him self-consciously. There a terrible second where she was sure he would shoot her with a cocky grin, the way he did at the very start of their relationship before they knew each other well.

But he didn't. There was the faintest twitch as if he was considering it. But then he just looked at her. No smile, no bullshit.

Emma shivered. His eyes were golden and warm and *far* too piercing. She'd forgotten how spellbinding he could be when he dropped those goddamn walls and focused entirely on her.

"And I know who you are," he said, his voice devastatingly soft. "Under all this."

"Under *what*?"

He nodded at her: arms crossed tight over her chest, her face twisted in a scowl.

"You're still the same sweet, passionate girl who uses anger to hide how much she cares," he said quietly. "The same girl who needs to unwind with Cool Whip and *Casablanca* after a long day. Who takes care of what's hers and fights for... for what she cares about."

Something brushed Emma's leg. She jumped, looking down to see his tail trailing over her knee. The scales were neat and shiny, just like always. He kept them pristine, just like his wings. She used to rub oil into his feathers and clip his scales. He probably got the help to do that now.

That gleaming tail curled around her thigh.

"You really should just come out and say it plain," he said. "I know you haven't been getting what you need."

Emma's cheeks heated. She wanted to think it was from indignation, but she knew better: it was the same old reason she got flustered when he got close. Like he was doing right now, his breath minty and warm as he leaned over the table.

"The hell do you know about my needs?" she asked, distantly impressed by how unaffected she sounded. Like there wasn't heat pooling between her legs. Like she wasn't pouring every ounce of willpower into not staring at his mouth.

Arthur smiled, soft and small and *knowing*. His right wing ducked down, feathers brushing her hot cheek.

Emma shivered. It was useless pretending she didn't. He could probably *smell* how wet she was, the keen-nosed bastard.

He grinned, all those sharp teeth on full display. "Want me to show you?"

SEVEN

Arthur waited, his breath frozen in his chest.

It was entirely possible he had misread this entirely. He hoped he hadn't. But twelve years was a long time, and she was *still* staring at him. Maybe she would throw the risotto in his face. Both bowls, for good measure. Grind the bread to crumbs in his mane and storm out into the snow and make him run out after her and argue until she let him fly her down the mountain.

She lunged, jarring the table so hard that risotto splattered over the tablecloth he'd found in the linen closet. Arthur barely noticed, too occupied with her hands tangling in his shirt, her mouth a blazing pressure against his. He'd forgotten what kissing her was like when she was angry at him, when he successfully taunted her into leaping on him instead of cussing him out. It was glorious. He huffed a laugh against her lips.

She immediately pulled back, glaring. "What? Is this funny to you?"

"No," he replied. "I just—"

Missed you. He clamped his jaw shut before he could say it. He'd started this to *stop* all the sincerity, not keep it going. To stop his stomach from doing that nervous squirming that had rarely happened since he left Claw Haven. And, he was starting to realize as she dug her fingers into his mane and pulled him back in, so he could make her smile.

He *loved* making her smile. He hadn't realized how much he missed it until he felt it against his lips. He'd dedicated most of his high school career to making her smile. Once or twice, he'd had the ludicrous thought that he was put on this earth to make Emma Curt smile.

He pulled her into his lap, sliding his hands up her smooth back. She smelled like coffee beans and, inexplicably, the same deodorant she wore in high school. *Berry Blast.* He nuzzled her neck, breathing in the scent he'd once known as much as his own.

"This isn't..." Emma paused, moaning as he pressed a careful bite to her collarbone. "This *isn't* a date."

"Never," he agreed. He rocked up against her, letting her feel his growing erection.

Her mouth dropped open, her face going hazy with desperation. She tried to cover it up, but it was too late. A low growl built in his chest, oddly possessive. She really *hadn't* been getting what she needed. He knew the town wasn't full of the best and brightest, but these idiots were really letting her go unsatisfied like this? What was Claw

Haven coming to? And just after he'd been grudgingly starting to admit it wasn't all bad.

He grabbed her ass and stood, heart jumping when her arms looped automatically around his neck. They'd done this before, after all. Muscle memory counted for a lot.

"Let me give you what you need," he said. "You don't have to be pissed off about it. Just tell me how you want it."

She blinked down at him. He was holding her up high, the way she liked.

"I thought you said you knew," she said breathily. "Admitting defeat so soon?"

He laughed, unable to stop it. "Right, I'm sorry. Marathon fucking with no foreplay, coming up."

He fell back onto the couch, dragging her with him. She landed in his lap with a yelp, which quickly turned into a moan as she ground down against his hardening cock.

"Like hell," she said. She tipped her head back, eyelids fluttering. "You have a condom, right?"

He nodded. "Still not a date," he added quickly when she glared at him. "I just like being prepared."

She smirked. For a second, he thought he caught a glimpse of something sad in it. Then she kicked her shoes off and leaned down, sucking his tongue into her mouth.

The rumble in his chest grew louder. He crushed her close, inhaling the heady scent tumbling off her in waves. He'd always liked making a girl feel good, but he hadn't had this narrow-minded drive in a *while*. He wanted to drive her fucking crazy. Show her what she'd been missing, sure, but also give her what she needed. No wonder she was strung so tight if she hadn't been getting good orgasms on the regular.

He peeled off her shirt, groaning as her breasts spilled out in front of him.

"Shit," he said. "I missed these."

He leaned in, teasing her nipples with his fangs. She startled, her grip tightening in his mane.

He grinned into her skin. "Have you fucked a chimera since me?"

"Not a lot of chimeras to fuck around here," she reminded him, grinding down into his lap. "Who am I going to roll around with, the *mayor*? No, *thank* you."

"Oh yeah, I heard Christopher got that role. He dropped by for a photo op yesterday. Good guy." Arthur undid her jeans and thrust a hand into her panties, luxuriating in her gasp as he circled her stiff clit. "Think he'd make you feel like this?"

She bit her lip, hips working. "He's hot," she managed with a stuttering laugh. "M-maybe I should've tried."

Arthur ignored the wave of jealousy that surged through him as he imagined it. It was ridiculous—Christopher was too mild-mannered, too put together, too *boring*—but it still made him clutch her tighter, dragging her jeans off so roughly he almost ripped the fabric.

She let out another startled laugh, cupping him over his slacks. "What about *you*, big boy? Kinda getting the vibe you haven't been getting what you need. Thought everybody was falling all over you in LA."

"They are," he said. "I'm just..."

He kissed her again, stopping whatever pathetic thing was about to stumble out of his mouth. What was *with* him tonight? Obviously, Emma was still knocking him off his game, but he didn't expect her to do it so *thoroughly*. Especially when she wasn't even trying, too distracted by lust to focus on tearing him down.

He thumbed rough circles on her clit, the way she liked. She whimpered, the noise setting a fire in his belly. All his senses were narrowing down into her: the sweat growing on her skin, the needy hitch of her hips, how she was getting less and less able to hide how much she needed it.

"God, you're gonna come already," he realized.

She pried her eyes open long enough to glare. But even that was shot through with desperation, her teeth digging into her lip so hard the skin turned white.

"It's okay," he said. "I want you to. I'll make you come however many times you want, you know I can. I've got you, just let go."

It was like relearning an old dance: touching her clit, teeth scraping lightly over her neck, his other hand working her nipple. Grinding against her thigh, letting her get excited about what was to come. How many times had they done this, trying to keep quiet in his upstairs bedroom or her car parked in the beach parking lot after dark?

"Fuck," she whispered. "Oh, fuck. *Arthur*."

His cock jerked helplessly in his briefs as she came, her whole body going rigid with it. Her hips spasmed, her mouth open on a silent moan as he worked her through it.

Arthur couldn't look away. She was so beautiful, naked and writhing on top of him. The look on her face was just as exciting as the first time he'd seen it, clumsy and triumphant in the backseat of her car.

She relaxed against him but only for a second. Then she was pulling at his shirt, her fingers trembling on the buttons.

"Stupid collar," she panted.

He knocked her hands out of the way and started yanking the buttons free. She abandoned the shirt gladly, reaching down to undo his pants.

"What was that about foreplay?" he asked hoarsely.

She ignored him, pulling his cock out. She stared at it, thumbing the tip where pre-cum was gathering, and her lips parted in a hunger that made Arthur shiver.

She looked up at him, eyes gleaming.

"Stay," she told him.

She climbed off the couch, dropping to her knees on the carpet. She took a second to shove the coffee table back, making an annoyed noise as she noticed the spilled risotto. Then she turned back, reaching up to her head. Sweeping her hair back, he realized as her hands swept through empty air and faltered on her pixie cut. Either she got that haircut recently, or it had been a while since she'd been on her knees for a guy.

Before he could ask which one it was, she leaned down and sucked the head of his cock into her mouth.

He groaned, wedging a knuckle between his teeth to muffle the sound. He had a list of approved sex noises, and these were getting decidedly out of control. He couldn't help it: she looked so fucking hot down there, with her head bobbing and eyes closed as she sucked. Sinking lower and lower, trying to take him into her throat.

He sunk a hand into her hair, ready to pull her off. Despite her steadfast determination, she could never get the hang of deepthroating. But sure enough, his cock nudged the back of her throat and kept going.

He choked on air. Emma gagged around his cock, throat fluttering. But still, she sunk lower and lower until her nose pressed into his wiry pubes.

"Holy shit," he rasped. "Emma, *fuck*."

Emma pulled off, coughing. She wiped her mouth.

"What?" she asked when he looked down at her in rapt disbelief.

"Nothing," he managed. "Uh. Proud of you. You were really frustrated you couldn't do it."

She snorted, wiping her puffy lips.

"I did think about texting you," she admitted. Then she sunk back onto his cock, taking him deep into her throat and swallowing hard.

His head thumped back against the couch, lost in the sensations. He wanted to laugh at the idea of her texting him: *hey hope movie stardom is going ok, also i finally deepthroated.*

What would he have even said to that? *Congrats, I knew you could do it*? Would he have felt the same weird mix of pride and sadness he felt right now, trying not to think about some guy he probably knew in high school coaxing his cock deeper down her throat, telling her what a good job she was doing?

His orgasm was coming up fast. He didn't have the excuse of a dry spell, but it didn't matter. She was glorious.

"Come here," he gasped. He hauled her back into his lap.

She slid her hands under his open shirt, scratching at his furry pecs. "Condom?"

He fumbled in his pocket, pulling his wallet out and resurfacing triumphantly with a foil packet. He ripped it open with his teeth and slid it on. She grasped him before he was even finished, angling herself over him.

He grabbed her hips. "Impatient."

She ran her tongue along his fangs and asked, "What happened to giving me what I needed, huh?"

"I will," he said. "I just wanted to hear you say it."

He thrust up, sinking into her in one smooth motion. She cried out, eyes slamming shut. Her hands tightened in his mane so hard it stung.

He paused. "Too much?"

She shook her head vigorously. Her eyes cracked open, staring down at him in something so much like wonder it took his breath away. He clenched her hips, pushing back up into her once more.

She moaned, devastatingly loud. For a moment, the world narrowed into her transcendent expression, the single line of sweat running down her chest, and the need to make her come again. He couldn't remember the last time he'd been so unfocused on his own pleasure during sex. He needed to make her feel good like he needed air.

Then her hands came down over his own, stilling his motion.

"My turn," she breathed. "Don't move, okay?"

He nodded, dazed.

She grinned, bright and blazing. The truest smile he'd gotten out of her since he walked into her cafe. Then she started bouncing in his lap, riding him for all she was worth.

His trimmed claws pressed into her hips. He heard himself growl, wings twitching against the couch. This wasn't where he thought this was going—he'd more pictured *him* pounding *her* into the couch—but he sure wasn't complaining. He shouldn't have expected anything more, he realized as he watched her bounce on his cock. Of course, she'd want the upper hand. For someone who was all about Arthur opening up, dropping the mask, and being *real*, she didn't like being vulnerable either.

It didn't stop it from feeling weirdly intimate. Even as he tried to focus on how incredible she felt around him —the delicious flush traveling down her cheeks and chest, her gorgeous tits jiggling in his face—he couldn't help but think about how *close* they were. How right she felt in his arms, which came up to circle her back as she rode him. He'd slept with so many women he couldn't count, but it had never felt as intimate as it was with Emma.

He let out a startled moan as she sunk her hands into the soft underside of his wings.

She slowed, her hands pausing. "No?"

"It's good," he admitted, rushed. "You can keep going, it's good."

She started riding him in earnest again, squeezing around him. It was heaven. It was torture. He only let the beauticians and makeup artists at them when he had to. He *definitely* didn't let anybody touch his wings during sex. Never mind that it was Emma's go-to move, the thing guaranteed to make him come apart. Emma's slim fingers traced his feathers, pressing past them to touch the skin. Reaching behind him, she traced the place where his back met his wings, forcing a truly pathetic noise out of his throat.

She giggled. She looked delighted, even triumphant.

"Really should've fucked a chimera while you were gone," she panted. "Think they'd all be so easy for me? One little tug on their tail—"

She wound his tail around her wrist, stroking his scales.

"—and you're begging for it," she continued.

He grinned. "I don't hear me begging. Kinda thought it'd be *you* begging."

"What do I have to beg for? I'm getting"—she stopped, mouth falling open on a high-pitched moan—"what I n-need."

"Fucking told you." He reached for her clit.

She slapped his hands away. "Hey! I said stay."

He huffed a laugh, settling his hands around the small of her back. "You got mean."

"I was always mean." She grinned down at him, digging her hands into the softest part of his wings once more.

He shuddered under her touch. He wanted to correct her—she was *never* mean, she just played the part. Maybe she had asshole tendencies, but it was all to cover that great big heart he'd brought up at dinner. It wasn't a line. He'd seen that big heart even before he knew her all that well. She always thought he'd gone after her because he couldn't stand someone not liking him, but it wasn't true. He'd gone after her because he'd seen that big heart, and he wanted to be worthy of it.

Her forehead dropped against his. Her motions were speeding up, getting jerkier. Arthur's blunt claws dug harder into her spine. He wanted nothing more than to flip her over and pound her until she screamed. But she'd told him not to, assured him it was what she needed. He'd said he'd give it to her, hadn't he? He promised. He kept *some* of his promises.

"Fuck," she whispered into his mane. "Fuck, *Arthur*. You feel..."

"You too," he groaned. He could feel himself twitching in the condom, the base swelling. It felt surprisingly like a knot. Which was *typical*. He hadn't knotted anybody since Emma. Of course, it would show up again now. It wasn't like he was pulling out and knotting his hand, either; it just didn't happen for him. He came and slid right out, easy as anything. But he could feel it now, the base of his cock bulging bigger and bigger. Wanting to lock them together like they did when they were teenagers.

He cursed his ridiculous cock, which couldn't sense that this wasn't *their* Emma, it was *ex-girlfriend* Emma, who wouldn't fucking appreciate being locked onto him any longer than it took to make her come. That being said, she always liked it. Sometimes she even begged for his knot.

"I'm gonna come," he said. "Can I knot you?"

The sound she made in response was so needy his wings spasmed, feeling sure she'd say yes. Then she shook her head.

"Make me come," she said. "Do *not* knot me."

He growled. He was honestly unsure if he could hold off much longer, especially with all the sinful sounds she was making. But she guided his hand to her clit, her hips stuttering as he rubbed her.

"Yeah," she sighed. "Fuck. Oh *fuck*. Arthur."

"Use me," he said, shaking with the effort of keeping his hips still. "Feel that? That's all for you. Come on my cock, baby."

For once, she did exactly what he told her. She went rigid, her mouth wet and puffy and open as she cried out. He worked her clit, just the tip, the way he knew she liked. Making it so intense until it was almost *too* intense, her face creasing up as she rode out the aftershocks.

She grabbed his wrist. "Okay. That's—that's enough."

He nodded, gripping her thigh desperately. There were faint dents on her hips from his trimmed claws; he bet there were matching ones in her back. Once she was littered with them, a constant studding of marks that would fade in a few days.

She looked down at their conjoined bodies with a breathless laugh.

"Oh, I can feel it starting. Gonna be a *big* one," she announced, swiveling her hips in a slow, tantalizing circle. "You want to knot me?"

"Yes," he panted, trembling with it. "Fuck, yeah, please."

She flashed her blunt teeth. "Told you I'd make you beg."

Then she climbed off of him, sitting on the couch beside him and leaning over to jerk him light and fast.

He groaned helplessly. Her hand felt good, but nowhere near as good as the hot clutch of her body. He leaned toward her, trying to catch her mouth. He needed her on top of him again, he needed her close, needed *more*—

She nipped his lip again. "You said you wanted to knot me. Do it already."

He was too close to do anything but obey. His wings arched as he came. Come shot over his stomach, catching in his fur and his shirt, which had never made it all the way off. It was so intense his eyes slammed shut, colors dancing under his eyelids. When he opened them again, his cock was soft except for the thick bulge at the base, pink and stiff.

Emma's breath hitched. She traced it idly with her thumb, the desire so obvious in her face that Arthur's heart leaped. She *did* want him to knot her. Even after all this time, she had wanted it, even if it meant they got stuck together for twenty minutes or even two hours like that one time in senior year.

She wiped a speck of come off her wrist and started to get up.

"Nope," he said instantly. He wrapped his arms around her bare waist and dragged her back into his lap.

She batted him half-heartedly. "I gotta shower."

"Shower later. Nap now." He lay down on the couch, pulling her on top of him.

She snorted. "Ugh. Since when are you *that* guy?"

"I've had a very long day," he said.

She twisted in his arms to give him a look. It obviously wanted to be stern, but she was too satisfied, her limbs loose against him even as she pulled back.

Arthur waited, wings curving around her. Trying to keep her close. At first, he thought she would insist, and he'd have to give in. He'd already gotten a hell of a lot more out of tonight than he thought he would.

Then she sighed, lying down against him. "Fine. Twenty minutes! Then you're flying me back down."

"You got it," he said.

She fell asleep before he did. He listened to her breathe, the furrow between her brows finally smoothing out in sleep.

"There we go," he murmured. He shifted against the couch. He was still covered in come and his knot was only just going down. He really should shower soon, but until then, he could let himself enjoy this. Emma Curt, in his arms once more. Probably for the last time.

He nuzzled her hair. She didn't smell like Berry Blast anymore. She smelled like sweat and come and *him*. It felt right. Righter than red carpets, righter than a hundred cameras pointed at him. He'd never felt more right than when he was holding Emma in his arms. His tail twisting between her legs, his wings tucked around her back.

He let his wings pull even closer, feathers brushing her back. Once, he thought he'd do this every night for the rest of his life.

His eyes burned. He blinked hard, alarmed, thinking of dust and allergies and then realizing that no, he was just tearing up. Ridiculous. He didn't cry outside of scenes. And even then, it was an elegant tear, something suitable for a charming, strong leading man.

Emma made a sleepy noise against his chest.

He closed his wings tighter.

EIGHT

Something tickled Emma's nose.

She pried her eyes open. Feathers clouded her vision, a sea of black and white. For just a moment, the sight relaxed her more. She'd woken up like this so many times. Arthur practically lived at her house for those last few years of high school.

Then reality set in, and Emma's relaxation was replaced by panic. She wasn't a teenager anymore. She was thirty-two goddamn years old, she owned a business, she hadn't talked to Arthur in years, and yet she was cocooned in his wings on the couch of his stupidly cozy cabin.

His arms were tight and solid around her, his tail still wrapped around her legs. She winced, trying to detangle herself. How could she be so stupid? She needed to get out of here—now. No matter how good it felt to be in his arms again.

She pulled his arm carefully off her torso.

He let out a sleepy growl, grip tightening. He nuzzled her hair, and she fought down the wave of butterflies that threatened to overwhelm her as she wondered how many models, actresses, and billionaires he'd given the same treatment. If they woke up feeling just as safe and held as she had.

She winced and pulled more determinedly.

He growled louder, disgruntled. Then his eyes slid open. They were blurry for a second, blinking hard. He focused on her, and the surprise in his face made Emma's hackles go up. She tensed, ready to snap back at whatever stupid thing he was going to hit her with.

Then he grinned, looking so genuinely pleased her guard went down.

"Hello," he said. He stretched, wings retreating from their squeezing grip. "What time is it?"

She checked her phone, which was in the pocket of her discarded jeans. "Almost nine."

The smile dropped off his face. "Really? Shit. We have to be on set in ten minutes."

He lifted her off his lap and stood, grimacing as he noticed the dried come in his chest fur.

"I'm going to take the world's shortest shower," he announced. "Time me."

"I'm fine, thanks." Emma scrounged for her bra and tried not to react as he looked over her nakedness. It had been a long time since a guy had seen her this naked. The last guy she slept with didn't even get her pants off, they just did hand stuff in the back of a car like they weren't fully grown adults with mortgages.

He put a hand on his hip, flashing her a toothy grin. "Want to conserve water and hop in the shower with me?"

Emma gathered up her jeans, pretending to think about it. "No."

She balled her clothes up against her stomach and waited for him to argue. But he just stood there, looking at her. Emma squirmed, fighting the urge to cover up her chest. It wasn't that she didn't *like* him looking at her; it just made her aware of how brazen she'd felt last night and how stupid she felt now.

Too fast for her to react, Arthur leaned in and plucked something off her cheek.

"Feather," he explained softly. He cleared his throat, dusting the fluffy down from his fingers. He was still smiling, but it was oddly bashful in a way that she hadn't seen since high school—which made zero sense. He probably picked feathers off people's cheeks all the time after rolling around with them on a yacht or a grand piano or sheets with a thread count she'd never heard of. Was he acting? He didn't seem like it, but maybe she'd gotten worse at reading him over the years.

"Anyway," he said. "I'm gonna..."

He hooked a thumb over his shoulder. Emma watched him go, then flopped back against the annoyingly comfortable couch, her clothes in her lap.

One night. She'd let herself have *one* night of something stupid and brilliant. She wouldn't do it again. He'd be gone in a week and a half, and she'd never have to see it again. The butterflies would fade, and so would the regret.

Life would go back to normal.

She took the second world's shortest shower after him, throwing on her clothes and shoving her damp hair under a hat. She took a second to sigh at her reflection, decided she didn't care if she looked like crap, and marched into the kitchen where the noise was coming from.

Arthur looked up. He was easing lids onto plastic takeout containers, which had been filled with last night's risotto. The bread was wrapped in a dishtowel, tied in a clumsy knot.

"Hey," Arthur said brightly. "Here's today's lunch."

He tossed it at her. She caught it, bewildered. She'd been expecting to get hit on some more and rushed out the door, not... leftovers. She tucked them in her handbag.

"I know you hate wasting food," he continued, sucking a speck of risotto off his finger. "Come on, we gotta go."

He led her outside, not bothering to lock the cabin door before he turned to her and held out his arms. "Up you get."

She stared at them warily, annoyed at the part of her that wanted to fling herself back into them and never let go.

"There's a car," she said, gesturing down the road. "Right?"

"Flying's faster." He clapped, arms coming out wider. "Come on."

She sighed and walked up, looping her arms around his neck. He picked her up easily, the cold already much more bearable when she was pressed up against his chest.

Seconds passed. Nothing happened. She looked up at him, cheeks heating when she saw he was watching her.

"What happened to being in a hurry?"

"We still are." His arms flexed around her, wings poised for flight. "Would you like to take me on a tour after the shoot ends?"

"Oh, would I *like* to," she said, automatic. "Thanks for giving me this golden opportunity—"

"You can just say no."

She fixed him with a dubious look. "I refuse to believe you haven't gotten one yet."

"I had offers," he admitted. "I want it to be you."

He said it so casually. And yet it made her traitorous heart clench.

She opened her mouth to say no. To say *hell* no. To say that last night was fun, but she wasn't about to dig herself deeper into the heartbreak that until a few days ago, she thought she had gotten over. She wasn't digging this hole any deeper.

"Fine," she said instead.

He beamed. "Great! I can't wait to see your argument for how this place is actually worth living in. Something tells me it's improved over the years."

"Claw Haven *is* worth living in," she snapped. "If you just—"

"Save it for tonight," he told her and took off.

She yelped, clinging. The icy wind stung her cheeks. She turned her face grudgingly into his mane, ignoring the pleased look on his face.

It didn't mean anything. Not the risotto or his continuous attempts to string her along.

He'll be gone by New Year's, she reminded herself and held him tighter.

He soared over the town, heading dangerously close to Main Street.

"You can drop me off a block away," she told him.

He hummed. Pretending to consider it, she realized and had to bite her cheek to hold back a laugh.

"Nope," he said, landing right outside Cozy Grotto Cafe.

Before Emma could decide whether to double back and pretend she was just coming in, a dozen heads swiveled to look at her through the glass—including but not limited to camera operators, his glamorous costar, Daisy and Hazel, Luna Musgrove, and extras who had known Emma her whole life and looked far too overjoyed to see Emma climbing out of her ex's arms.

Emma smiled tightly. Great.

Arthur held the door open for her. "After you."

She ignored him, adjusting her handbag and walking in. Some of the camera crew were getting back to work, but everyone who already knew Emma was taking their sweet time looking away. Thankfully Daisy and Hazel were stuck behind the counter talking to the director, but Luna Musgrove made an immediate beeline toward her, looking positively delighted.

"Helloooo," Luna said, blonde hair bouncing. "You look great! Are those last night's clothes?"

Emma tugged her into the corner, out of the way of the crew and the nosey townsfolk. It wouldn't help if there were any vampires or werewolves around, but Emma hoped that her reputation was enough to make them butt out of her private conversations.

"Do me a favor and shush," Emma told her. "Why are you here?"

"What, I can't drop by the most exciting thing that's happening all winter?" Luna fluttered her eyelashes. She looked... way too knowing, Emma realized. Suspiciously knowing.

"Luna," Emma said gravely. "What did you do?"

Luna linked her hands together under her chin. "Whatever do you mean?"

Emma tugged her hands back down. "Luna!"

Luna laughed. "Nothing! I just pointed him in Heath's direction. Who knew the guy could cook as well as bake? Did you like the risotto?"

"It was fine." Emma adjusted her handbag strap, listening to the leftover containers clack together. "You're an asshole."

"You love it," Luna said breezily, turning to watch the crew set up.

The makeup artists had gotten to Arthur, brushing out the mane he'd avoided during this morning's shower as they led him out back to the wardrobe. Emma prickled. She could never do that; she hated strangers touching her. But he seemed so calm, letting them peel his lips back to examine his fangs as the door swung shut behind them.

Luna leaned in, her glossy hair tickling Emma's chin. "Is he very different than when you knew him?"

Emma snorted, folding her arms. "No. Same annoying, self-obsessed chimera."

"Sure." Luna waved a dismissive hand. "But he's got layers, right? You wouldn't have dated him otherwise."

Emma didn't reply. Sometimes she thought she'd imagined it all: the sweet moments, the times when he dropped his mask and was just... *Arthur*. No bells and whistles, no flashy lights. The deep emotions he pretended not to have were finally seeping through.

He'd stopped bringing up LA. She thought he was happy with their life together. Then he ambushed her on Christmas Eve to tell her he had an audition in the New Year and he wanted her to come with him. But when it became clear that she wasn't, he just... stopped begging. His face had closed off. No tears, no regret. Just a mild smile.

Maybe it's better this way. You won't be holding me back anymore.

Then he'd left. He rode out of town in the car his parents bought him and never looked back. He hadn't called. Granted, she had screamed at him not to, but he would've if he wanted. The next time she saw him, it was a movie poster they hung up in the movie theater. This was before they started showing more than two movies a year, so Emma was forced to look at his stupid face every day as she drove to work for six goddamn *months*. Then again when his next movie came out, and the next. His smug smile blared down at her from the poster, all charm and fangs. Looking at some girl like she was the whole world.

"He's a good actor," Emma said flatly.

"Well." Luna nudged her. It wasn't hard, but it was enough to make Emma grit her teeth. Luna was a friend, but they weren't *that* close.

Luna continued, "I'm just glad you two—"

"Just stop," Emma snapped. "I know you get off on gossip, but get your nose out of my personal life. Okay?"

Luna blinked, surprised. Emma hadn't snapped at her since the first day they met when Luna playfully batted her arm one too many times.

"Ooookay," Luna said quietly. "Noted."

Emma was still scowling when Arthur came out of the backroom, dressed in an entirely different suit, an apron tied around his waist. He paused to let a makeup artist run one last comb through it, then headed over to his mark. His costar—who Emma belatedly learned was called Jennifer, a Hollywood nepo baby who rose to fame through her famous director dad—wiggled her fingers at him as they took their places behind the counter.

A hush fell over the cafe.

"Okay," Rusty called. "Everybody ready? Three. Two. One. And... action!"

Daisy started fake-taking an order at the till. Hazel bustled around, fake-making a coffee. Behind them, the camera crew zoomed in on Jennifer and Arthur as they stacked mugs onto a shelf.

The cafe was quiet enough for Emma to hear every word.

"Pretty cramped behind here," Arthur said. "You don't get uncomfortable?"

"I don't know," Jennifer replied. "I'm getting used to it."

She bumped her hip against his. He grinned at her, eyes crinkling. Emma's grip tightened around her handbag as she remembered kissing those stupid laugh lines last night. The marks he'd left on her twinged: blunt claw marks on her hips, her thighs, her back. She used to touch them every morning in the shower, giddy and hot. There had been a glimpse of that this morning, heat curling in her gut as she ran her hands down her soapy thighs. The marks would be gone soon.

Good riddance, she thought. But it didn't sound convincing, even in the privacy of her own head. She'd missed him. His cock, sure. But also the way he saw right through her. She thought she'd been doing a good job hiding that she hadn't gotten any for a while. Then he'd showed up and ruined that. It had taken him a while to learn to see past her anger and see what she was hiding under it, but apparently, he still had the knack. She just hoped he didn't see how pathetic she felt when she thought about how easily he left. How much she wanted him around, even as she raged at him. How much she'd missed him despite everything.

"I can teach you a thing or two," Jennifer said.

Emma blinked. She'd obviously missed a few lines of dialogue while she spaced out. She hadn't realized how hungry she was. She had barely eaten dinner, and she hadn't had breakfast yet.

"I bet you can," Arthur said, voice low.

They were standing so *close*. Emma fidgeted as they stared into each other's eyes, all those cameras trained on them. How the hell did they do this with so many people watching? She wasn't even in the shot and it was making her skin crawl.

It's not real, she reminded herself as Arthur and Emma drew closer. It didn't help. She couldn't stop watching his eyes, so big and soft, watching her like she was everything. The same way he'd looked at her, once.

Arthur leaned in. Jennifer smiled into the kiss, her pleased hum easily audible even from all the way across the cafe.

Emma clenched her handbag, the plastic containers pushing hard against each other. It was fake. That was what Arthur did, he faked it until he got what he wanted, no matter who got hurt because of it.

What the hell was she doing here? This was never going to end well. Better to end the fling now, after one night, than let him drag her along for another week.

"Cut," Rusty yelled. "Alright, let's do that one again.

Jen, this time could you try that last line with a bit more pizzazz?"

Emma wasn't sticking around for this. She headed quietly for the door.

"Em?" Luna said.

Emma ignored her. Her eyes burned as she strode out onto the snowy street, which was once again bustling with shoppers. It was a twenty-minute walk to her house. The streets had been cleared for most of the trek, but the last stretch would soak her jean cuffs yet again.

"Emma!"

Emma groaned and kept walking.

Arthur caught up fast. She heard him give a brief greeting to someone who was no doubt staring at the big fancy movie star right here in their podunk little town before he was behind her. Not touching her—not this time.

Emma was grateful. Emma was annoyed. Emma wanted that big hand to close on her shoulder and turn her around, wanted it to sink into her hair, wanted it to warm her cheek like he'd done last night.

"You have a scene to finish," she reminded him, still walking.

"They can wait," Arthur said and ducked in front of her. "Where are you off to?"

"Home." She tried stepping around him. He let her, falling into step beside her.

"Are you okay?" he asked.

"I'm fine."

He snorted. "You're upset."

She didn't look at him. She could see him smiling out of the corner of her eye, that coaxing smile he pulled up when he could tell someone was mad and was hoping he could charm them out of it.

"I need new clothes," she said.

"You look great!"

"Well, then, I need a nap."

"Okay," Arthur said, laughing at the obvious lie. "When should I expect you back for the grand tour?"

She whirled to face him. People streamed around her, ignoring her, staring at the incredible Arthur Pineclaw who came to a stop beside her. Still smiling, still beautiful, the kind of beauty that demanded attention. No wonder they loved him so much in the big city. No wonder they plastered him all over their screens when he looked like that—when he could look at people the way he'd looked at Jennifer in the cafe, the way he'd looked at Emma last night. It took a special talent to make you believe in a romance with one look.

Emma swallowed, trying to drag back the anger. "This is a bad idea. This whole thing was a bad idea. I should never have met up with you last night; we shouldn't have—"

"Whoa, hey." Arthur stepped closer, voice lowering. "Where is this coming from?"

She threw her arms up. "Gee, I don't know! Christmas, twelve years ago?"

He was still smiling, watching her with something too close to hope—that movie star smile fading into something scarily genuine. Then it grew, turning back into that smile he used with paparazzi.

"Emma," he started. Too smug, too *knowing*. She hated that he knew her so well, even after all this time. "Come on. We had a great time last night. Don't ruin it with this thing you do."

"Thing?" Emma hissed. "What *thing*, Arthur?"

Arthur hesitated. His smug smile wavered, but only for a moment.

"You feel something you don't like," he said slowly. "And then you get mad because it's *easier* than feeling whatever's under it."

Emma clenched her teeth so hard her jaw ached. A thousand fleeting conversations with her parents and her short-lived therapist ran through her head at once.

"I don't do that," she mumbled.

"You *do*," he said. "You were getting better at *not* doing it. I hoped you'd be over it by now."

Emma swallowed. He'd said something the other day about her *liking* certain waves of anger. She'd lain in bed that night, fuming, determined that he was just getting under her skin. Was this something he actually believed about her? Something he'd believed even back when they were together? She didn't like anger. She didn't rely on it to cover stuff up, she just... got angry sometimes. The world was frustrating. That wasn't *her* fault.

A strange, shaky feeling came over her. It felt a lot like a realization. Then rage rushed to cover it, as blinding and reliable as ever.

"Yeah," she snapped. "I hoped you'd be different, too.

That you'd stop with all your empty, pandering *bullshit*. So, apparently, we're both disappointed!"

She pushed past him.

"Emma," he tried.

He reached for her. She dodged it, whirling on him.

"*Don't*. Just go back and finish the scene, alright? Don't let me *hold you back*."

It should've felt good, throwing that back in his face. Turning his own last words against him. Turning her back, the same way he'd done to her all those years ago.

But it was a hollow victory. The anger dissipated as soon as it came, too stuck on how the smile had fallen off his face for good when she left him there. He'd been trying to pull it back up, but she'd seen it.

He *had* missed her. That part was true, at least.

NINE

Arthur did not *slump*.

It was trained in him at a very young age that presentation was everything. His parents even gave him etiquette training, which would have gotten him teased if he was anyone else. Fortunately, Arthur had enough charisma to make telling the other small-town kids about the proper way to use a shrimp fork look cool.

The point was that he didn't slump. But he was coming pretty damn close as he leaned against the bar at Sour Claw, which was one of the only places that hadn't changed since he left. Granted, he'd only been in here a few times. He even brought a fake ID as a teen, which was utterly useless since everybody knew him. The bartender let him drink anyway. They hadn't been too strict with carding back then.

"I just can't believe she's still not over it," Arthur complained as he nursed his second whiskey of the night.

"She isn't answering my texts. She hasn't even been at the shoot for days!"

Rusty shook his head, tapping away at his phone. "Like I said, man. Crazy."

"Haha," Arthur said, ignoring the itch of irritation that rose every time Rusty said something like that about Emma. "She's not CRAZY. She's just... dramatic. She feels things really deeply."

He took another drink, wincing at the subpar taste. He hadn't had whiskey this cheap in almost a decade. He thought he'd been misremembering how crappy it was. Apparently not.

He sighed, wings drooping. "I don't know, I thought we had something. But then she throws that in my face! I was nineteen, what was I supposed to do, *not* go? And hello, it worked out great! I just... *ugh*. She's always yelling!"

"Yell back for once," Rusty suggested, still tapping away. "I'd pay to see that. The closest I've come to seeing you yell is that time Henry Roarson kept spilling wine in your best car."

"He was doing it on purpose," Arthur reminded him. "It's not *my* fault he felt snubbed by the awards people."

"Not your fault you're the better actor," Rusty agreed.

Arthur clinked their drinks together. Rusty had been the one to suggest they head to a bar after Arthur admitted he was off his game today, and Arthur was grateful for it. He didn't have a lot of people who he could confide in nowadays. Rusty was a rare example of a genuine friend, which was the only reason Arthur kept talking. With anyone else, he'd change the subject, get them talking about the movie or a future holiday or something fun that happened at a party last year. But Rusty was his friend, a *real* friend, and Arthur needed that right now.

"I just..." Arthur sighed. "She keeps getting mad like that's gonna hide all the crap behind it. I need to fix this."

"Why?" Rusty muttered. Then he looked up, seemingly surprised that he'd said it out loud. "I mean, sure. Whatever it is, you can fix it."

Arthur nodded distractedly. Any other day, it would've been about making her like him so he could stop feeling bad. But somehow the idea had lost its luster. He wanted to make her happy so she was happy. No strings, no ulterior motives. Hell, he'd even be fine with her being pissed off at him if it made her happy, which was... a surprise. But he could see how much hurt she hid behind all that anger. He had another week before they headed back to LA on Christmas Eve. That would have to be enough time.

A throat cleared behind him.

Arthur turned.

Nick Wicker waved at him. The orc looked almost exactly the same as he did when Arthur last saw him: blunt fangs sticking up from his bottom lip, messy hair, and green skin stained with motor oil. Jasper Dawn stood beside him, pale as ever, his vampire fangs out.

Arthur beamed. "The Terrible Two! Still getting up to trouble at Sour Claw, huh?"

"Always," Jasper said wryly. He was smirking, which wasn't uncommon. Most of the memories Arthur had of him were of Jasper smirking or looking deeply bored. They'd been in different years at high school, but Arthur had seen him around at parties or slouching through the halls, twisting that long black hair around his white fingers.

"We love your stuff," Nick said, hands stuffed deep in his pockets. "Well. Some of it. *Just Kitten Around* was a fart in a jar, but everybody has flops."

"We were wondering if we could get an autograph from the great big movie star," Jasper drawled. "Care to oblige?"

"Love to." Arthur took the napkin Nick shoved at him and scribbled his name. "Want one each?"

"Sure," Nick gushed. "Want to play a game of pool? I still suck, so it's an easy win."

"He does suck," Jasper agrees. "He doesn't come here often enough."

Nick snorted, digging his big green elbow into Jasper's narrow waist. "Sorry, the stress of the hospital job doesn't force me to come here and drown my sorrows."

Arthur looked up. "Oh? You're a doctor?"

"Janitor," Jasper corrected, fangs flashing once again. "Nick's just being a dick."

Nick coughed into a meaty fist. "Anyway. Pool?"

Arthur paused, pen trailing off at the end of the

second autograph on another napkin. He could play pool. Or he could go and follow an idea that just popped into his mind upon seeing his old classmates: there was another old classmate he could hit up.

"Some other time," he said, handing the napkins over with a smile. He patted Rusty on the back and eased off his chair, flexing his wings in preparation. He'd done a lot of flying since he arrived in town, so he might as well keep the streak going.

Rusty turned. "Where are you off to?"

"I gotta go see a guy about some flowers," Arthur called back and strode out into the chilly parking lot.

Joshua Haberdash was closing up the shop when he landed.

"Whoa," Joshua said, jumping. The keys clattered to the sidewalk next to Arthur's polished boots. "Damn."

"Sorry about that," Arthur said, stooping.

"No, I got it." Joshua lunged, grabbing them before Arthur could touch them. "Hiya."

"Hiya," Arthur echoed. He eyed the shop hopefully. The lights were off, but he'd talked people into closing late for him even before he got his face on billboards. "Do you get a lot of business for apology flowers?"

Joshua pushed that annoying bit of hanging fur out of his eyes. "Yes. Other than birthdays and dates, apology flowers are my most popular kind of sale."

"Great!" Arthur fluffed up his mane pointedly,

hoping that Joshua would take the hint and invite him inside. "Are you good at getting girls to forgive you?"

Joshua's wet nose twitched. He looked confused. Arthur doubted he'd ever done anything bad enough to warrant a serious apology.

"No?" Joshua said, sounding uncertain. Then, as Arthur was about to try something else: "But I'm good at listening. In the warm, though. My fur isn't *that* thick."

Arthur sighed in thanks as Joshua closed the shop door behind them. It was practically toasty in here—as toasty as a flower shop could be, anyway. It was possible Arthur had been out in the cold too long.

"Okay," Joshua said, adjusting a display of roses. "What happened?"

Arthur started in on his explanation. Joshua nodded attentively, and Arthur realized he was flattered. He was used to people going above and beyond for him, but he was pretty sure he didn't charm Joshua into anything. He was just a sweet guy. Even in high school, Joshua had been known for being outrageously kind. Stupidly so, one might argue. He got made fun of for it. But Arthur couldn't help but admire him a little, even if he did occasionally join in on the teasing.

"So," Arthur said when he finished. "What do you think I should do?"

He expected the minotaur to repeat that he didn't have much experience in this. But Joshua replied immediately.

"Leave her alone," Joshua said. "That's what she asked. Right?"

"But I don't *want* to," Arthur protested. He couldn't stop himself from wincing as he said it. It sounded perfectly sensible until it came out of his mouth. He started to try again, to tell Joshua he genuinely wanted Emma to be happy, but Joshua was already talking.

"Okay," he said slowly. "What *do* you want?"

"I want..." Arthur said before hesitating. He could feel a growl deep in his chest. He did it so rarely that it felt foreign to feel the growl surface outside of a scene where someone had told him to do it or when he was too out of his head to notice. But here it was, ripping out of him.

"I want her to stop fighting me on this," he snarled, pacing. "I want her to *let* me make her happy. I know I could do it if she just *let* me. I could air out all that shit she's been keeping locked up. I could make her *like* me again."

"So tell her that," Joshua said simply, surprisingly undeterred by the growling. Arthur remembered him being freaked out when anybody growled in school.

"And if she still wants you to leave her alone, then put up with it," Joshua continued. "Can't make someone like you."

Arthur laughed, narrowly missing knocking over a vase of lilies as he whirled to pace another length of the floor. "Yes, I can! I was voted the most likable man in Hollywood last year! Directors love me. My costars love me. The *paparazzi* love me. Do you *know* how hard it is to keep smiling when they're in your face, asking the rudest goddamn questions? *Everyone* likes me except her. She just—"

He flexed his flat claws, fangs gnashing. "She scrapes all of my *charming* away! And if she doesn't like what she sees under that, then—"

He stopped, mortified. What was he doing, airing his personal shit to Joshua Haberdash? He barely knew the guy. He could practically hear his parents' voices. His mother saying *Don't burden other people with your worries, dear. It's unseemly.* And his father, telling him to cut it out. They never shouted, never raged. But their tones would get stiff and uncomfortable, both of them averting their eyes whenever he dared to get upset or voice an emotion that they didn't want to deal with. Which was most of them. Arthur had learned very early on that if he wanted people to be happy with him—which was of utmost importance—he had to stuff any negative emotion behind a smiling mask. Luckily for him, he was good at it. Most of the time he forgot those emotions were there, and if he couldn't, he had a *very* convincing smile.

He pulled it up, ready to change the subject. But Joshua—the soft touch that he was—was already speaking.

"I tried to make people like me," he admitted. "When I was a kid. It only made them tease me more. They knew what I was doing."

"Should've gotten better at acting."

Joshua chuckled. "We can't all be charming, I guess.

Anyway, it took me a while to realize that worthwhile people will like you for you. You don't have to be something you're not. And if other people don't like it, who cares? As long as you have your people. And as long as YOU like you. Right?"

He tugged anxiously on the lank hair hanging over his eyes. Arthur had to give it to him: it was a pretty decent speech up until that weak ending.

"Sure," he said. "I just..."

He stopped. He couldn't think of anything to say except the ugly truth: he had never liked himself more than when he was with her. No, that was a lie. She made him uncomfortable sometimes, made him squirmy and shaky and embarrassed. He'd never felt as *complete* as he did with her after all the shaking and embarrassment was over. Once upon a time, he'd really believed she made him *better*. Made him *real*. She saw him, even when he tried to hide.

Nobody had really seen him since.

He cleared his throat. "Anyway. Apology flowers. I'd ask if you have wisteria—"

"We don't have that, sorry."

"No, I know," Arthur said hastily. "Trust me, that's... that's good."

He swallowed, forcing himself not to think of wraparound porches and deck chairs he once thought he'd grow old on.

"Anyway," he said, forcing a smile. "What do you suggest?"

· · ·

He knocked on Emma's door twenty minutes later, easing his grip on the bouquet he was holding. He kept bending the stems, the tissue paper crackling in his grip.

His heart lurched as he heard Emma's voice. He smoothed his mane, pulling up what he hoped was a relaxed smile.

"—don't know," Emma said as her voice came closer. "One second, I'm there."

The door opened. Emma froze. She had her phone to her ear. She was wearing a baggy pair of sweatpants and an even baggier Christmas sweater, more ugly than the first one. There was a smudge of Cool Whip on her cheek that Arthur itched to lick off.

He forced the impulse away. They were going to *talk* this time. Really sort things out.

"Hi," Arthur said. He lifted the white tulips Joshua had given him. "These are for you. I was wondering if you'd be interested in a tour?"

Her eyes narrowed. "I'm not—"

"I'll be the guide," he said hastily.

Emma's eyes narrowed further. Arthur could feel himself sweating. Standing here under Emma's keen gaze was somehow more taxing than all the flying he'd done today.

Emma put the phone back toward her mouth. "Never mind, Daisy. Gotta go." She shoved her phone into her sweatpants pocket. "*You* want to take *me* on a tour?"

"Yes! I'm a little out of date, but I'm a fast learner." The tissue paper crinkled in his grip. He forced his fingers to loosen, hoping she didn't notice. "Look. I'm... sorry. We didn't get much of a chance to talk... before."

"Didn't we? Mr. Let-me-show-you-what-you-need?"

"*You* kissed *me*," he reminded her. Then, when she started to roll her eyes: "No, that doesn't matter. I wanted to tell you I—I missed you. And maybe you're right, maybe we shouldn't have..."

He stopped. He didn't regret it. But it was obvious she did, standing there stiff and barefoot, her arms crossed tight over that Christmas sweater that was so awful it came back around to being cute.

He braced himself. She wanted him to drop his mask, so he was going to try.

"I want us to get along," he admitted in a rush. "To be civil, at least."

Her jaw clenched. For a moment, he thought he'd fucked it up. That he should've laid the blame on himself a little harder, *really* played the martyr.

The door slammed shut.

Arthur swallowed the sudden lump in his throat. He hadn't realized how badly he wanted her to say yes until right now. How much he cared what she thought of him. He'd been torn apart those first few months in LA, constantly agonizing over a phone number he never let himself dial.

He turned, tail drooping between his legs. He gave it an annoyed flick, holding it up in the neutral position he'd trained it into. He'd been so good about not reacting with his tail, why was it playing up so much since he got back to Claw Haven?

The door swung open.

Arthur whipped back around, ears pricking up. Emma stepped out onto the ramp, stuffing her feet into a pair of weathered boots, a scarf dangling haphazardly around her neck.

"Fine," she said. "But I'm driving."

TEN

Emma had to give it to him: he was dedicated to the bit.

She pointed her pumpkin spice latte at a nearby store. "And what's that?"

"That," Arthur said after a pause, "is obviously a... craft store."

She hummed into the plastic lid. "Close! Pottery."

"Pottery?" He squinted. "Huh. Cute. As I was saying, yet another wonder that is Main Street. And up on these lampposts, we have the ye olde Christmas decorations, which have apparently changed in the last twelve years."

"Not so old anymore," Emma agreed, eyeing the green tinsel. The street was less crowded now, most of the shoppers and holiday-goers having retreated to the inn for the evening. Emma was grateful. They could walk without bumping into anyone, and only one person had asked Arthur for an autograph so far.

"And here we have the bakery," Arthur continued, gesturing with his wing. "Now run by one Heath Astarot, who once puked fire after one too many Jäger-bombs at my sixteenth birthday party."

"And burned a hole in the hallway room carpet," Emma laughed. "I forgot about that! I have to bring that up next time I go in for a muffin."

"I'm sure he'll appreciate it," Arthur said. He grinned at her. Every time he made her laugh, he'd give her this look that made it hard to stop smiling. And she was *trying*. The problem was the more he talked to her, the harder it got to remember why she was trying so damn hard.

It was... *fun*. He was witty and bright and delightful, and he was so obviously trying to get on her level. Letting her make fun of him, being wrong on purpose so she could correct him. Making her feel at ease.

"And the bookshop," Arthur announced, pointing with another wing flourish. "Still run by that old one-winged dragon whose name I can never remember and who once yelled at me for picking up an art book off a tall shelf. And a chocolate shop run by Joshua's hedgehog cousin! She seems lovely when she gets past the stuttering."

A dragon soared overhead with a whooping human strapped to his belly.

"And, of course, we can't forget the dragon tours," Arthur continued, craning his head to watch the dragon swoop down toward the tour offices. "I have to say, I did *not* expect to run into those guys during my morning fly the first day I was here. *That* was a fun midair conversation."

Emma chewed her cheek to stop a smile. She took another sip of the pumpkin spice latte he'd brought her from Creature Comforts at the start of this "tour." She needed to teach her girls how to do more holiday specials. Daisy only knew a couple, and these tourists kept coming up with the wildest shit they insisted was all the rage back home. And she'd be happy if Hazel mastered *any* drink, let alone a holiday special. Maybe by this time next year, she'd have a handle on a basic latte.

"And," Arthur continued, pointing both wings for extra emphasis. "The movie theater, which now shows—"

"More than two movies a year," Emma finished. "We were very excited when they expanded."

"I bet." Arthur stared up at the poster, which showed his own face beaming out of him. It was the comedy, *Just Kitten Around*, which Emma privately thought he wasn't too proud of. Every time someone brought it up, it took him that extra moment to smile, like he was bracing himself against an onslaught of embarrassment. He always got like that over roles he thought he hadn't done well—mostly plays, back when she knew him. Once in middle school, she'd congratulated him on being the lead in the Christmas play and he'd told her that his performance was terrible and that he'd do better next year.

He flexed his wings as if shaking off a thought. Then he turned, taking in Main Street with a surprisingly genuine smile.

"You still can't get an Uber," he said. "Or noodles after 8 p.m. Or a nightlife. Or museums. But it's a hell of a lot less boring than it was twelve years ago."

"It was fine back then," Emma defended, tugging her scarf tighter. "It's just better now. Except for all the tourists."

"Aren't they the only reason your cafe didn't go under?"

"Yes," Emma admitted grudgingly. "But they're so annoying. And they're *everywhere*."

He shrugged. "Think of them like fans! You'd be nowhere without them. Even if they do sometimes make you want to find a dark corner to hide in."

"Oh?"

"One of them mailed me a voodoo doll of myself."

She shuddered.

"I don't open the fanmail anymore," he said happily. He started leading her past Main Street, the shops thinning back out into neighborhoods. "So! What are you doing for Christmas? I haven't seen your parents anywhere."

"They're on a cruise. Sailing around the Mediterranean, stopping to sunbathe on beaches. So I'm doing Christmas solo." She kicked a rock, watching it roll into the snow at the side of the cleared road. "What about yours? Cruise? Ski trip?"

"Norway," he replied. "And I find it hard to believe you have to be *alone*. Luna said she invited you up to the inn. Not in the mood for a big wolfy Christmas?"

"Sounds a bit loud for me," she admitted. "I have a

lot of invites, but... I don't know. Might just stay home and watch movies."

He hummed. It was a strange hum, considering and soft. She glanced over just in time to see him look away, examining his trimmed claws with great interest.

Emma went cold. Did he think she was sad, being alone on Christmas? He probably had a party full of people waiting for him when he got back to LA on Christmas morning. Why didn't she lie and say she was going to Luna's? Or *worse*, did he think she was angling for him to stay to keep her company? Ugh, that was pathetic.

She blurted out the first thing that came to mind. "Did you know they took *Minotaur's Mistletoe* off every streaming service?"

"Every streaming service," he repeated after a too-long beat. "No."

"*Every* one," she confirmed, grabbing an easy frustration and running with it. "My parents and I had to pirate it and press play at the same time like it was 2011! I can't keep track of what they're taking off those streaming sites anymore. I was so excited to curl up with a hot chocolate and virtually watch a Christmas classic with my parents, but could they give us that? No! We had to fuck around on pirating websites for an hour while I talked them through what a torrent was and how to get it past the cruise's Wi-Fi allowances!"

Arthur didn't reply.

She risked a look over. He was watching her with an

expression so soft that he hastily tried to cover it up, averting his gaze to his coffee cup this time.

"Call me crazy," he said, thumbing the plastic lid. "But I think you miss your parents. *Minotaur's Mistletoe*, that's, what... day six on your pre-Christmas movie list?"

Emma groaned. "Ugh. Of course, you remember that."

"Hard to forget!" He tugged at his chin fur, humming hard. "Let's see... *A Chimera Christmas Carol. It's A Wonderful Gargoyle Life. Die Hard Harpy*, I always appreciated that. You guys are keeping it going while they're on the cruise?"

She rolled her eyes. "We watched it over Zoom, okay? Is that too twee for you?"

"No. It's... sweet." He cleared his throat, flashing his fangs cheerily. "And how *are* your folks?"

"They're the same. And yours?"

"Good. As far as I can tell." Arthur's wings drew closer with the slightest twitch. It was a self-soothing technique, which he'd tried to stop himself from doing in high school. Apparently, it still seeped through.

Emma asked, "When did you last see them?"

Arthur paused, genuinely thinking about it. "Five years ago, I think."

Five years. That was a lot of birthdays, Christmases, and movie launches they missed.

"Really? It's not like you can't afford flights," she joked.

"I know. We're just all so busy."

Emma frowned. "Didn't they retire? I thought that was why they moved out of Claw Haven. To retire overseas."

"Busy retirees." He scratched his ear, another self-conscious tic he tried to ditch in high school. He'd always avoided talking about his parents. They were never cruel, as far as Emma knew. They were just... absent. He'd been politely bewildered by how involved Emma's parents were in her life, driving her to track meets, making pancakes with her on Sundays, and watching movies after everyone got home. He was equally bewildered by their initial dislike of him, unable to tell if his affections toward Emma were real or not.

When he kept laying it on thick even after he won them over, she'd assumed he was just sucking up to them. But it quickly became apparent that he just really liked having parental figures around. When his parents missed his graduation due to another one of their overseas holidays, Emma's parents cheered when Arthur's name was called and paid for his celebration dinner. They even made him a graduation cake to sit next to Emma's. It was the closest any of them had ever come to seeing Arthur cry.

"I was surprised your parents went without you," Arthur continued.

"They wanted to buy me a ticket. Can you imagine *me* on a cruise?"

Arthur laughed. "You'd spend most of it in your cabin avoiding everyone. I bet, ah—"

He stopped. They'd just turned the corner, and

Emma had a fleeting moment of confusion before she followed his gaze and everything clicked horribly into place.

They were standing in front of the house they had been planning on buying when they were teenagers. Half the house had a new coat of paint, fresh white that turned into that crusty yellow they both hated halfway around the house. The porch had a railing now, and the ivy had been torn away. Emma walked past here all the time, and she'd trained her eyes to avoid this house. It was almost second nature now.

Emma swallowed against a sudden rush of fury. Had he brought her here on purpose, trying to get a response? He looked too shocked for this to be anything but a genuine mistake.

Arthur's voice was raspy as he said, "It looks better. Not perfect, but better. Who bought it?"

"Nobody. Technically, it's abandoned." Emma crossed her arms tighter over her chest, determinedly not looking at the porch they promised they'd spend summer mornings on. "The mayor has been working on it with Jackson."

"Who?"

"The old dragon who fixed your gutters in high school and taught my parents how to make birdhouses."

"Right," Arthur said distantly, still staring up at the house. "Birdhouse guy."

"Anyway, they've been working on it. Easier to get more people to move here when the houses are ready to go. Not everyone wants a fixer-upper."

Arthur nodded. He was still staring at the porch, claws denting his latte, his tail swishing behind him. She'd seen his tail swish more than ever in those weeks leading up to their last Christmas together. Whenever she'd asked about it, he'd insisted everything was fine. She should've known.

Emma stepped back. "We should... get on with the tour."

"Right," Arthur said. "Tour. Sure."

For a second he didn't move. He just stood there, tail thrashing, the rest of him scarily still. Then he turned to her so fast a feather jolted out of his wing.

"Come to LA with me," he blurted.

Emma blinked. Part of her expected him to break out in a grin, those damned laugh lines creasing as he told her this was all a cruel practical joke that was being live-streamed on his Instagram as they spoke. But he just stood there, his tail stilling. He'd finally noticed and put a stop to it—like he stopped any display of genuine emotion.

"What?" Emma finally managed.

"Just to visit," he said, a strange smile tugging at his lips. "You'll like LA, I promise! I can fly you back to Claw Haven whenever you get tired of it..."

Emma stared at him, appalled. Her eyes were burning again, a pit opening in her chest. Fury rushed in to fill it, fiery and welcoming.

"What the *fuck* are you doing?" she exploded. "You think you can just swan in here with your—your suit and your stupid fucking sunglasses and ask me to uproot my life?"

"Just for a visit," he said, perilously close to begging. "Come on. I'm—I'm trying, okay? Dropping the mask. But you have to do it too. You have to *open up*, not just hide under the anger."

"I'm not *hiding*," she yelled. "I'm just angry! How dare you ask me that? Have those LA fur creams leaked into your brain and turned you crazy?"

"Emma." His smile was brittle and desperate, none of the charm that had earned him his awards, his mansions, and his fame. Just Arthur, being honest, *finally*. And breaking her goddamn heart.

Emma's breath hitched. She wanted to cry. She *refused* to cry in front of him, the selfish bastard. She reached for the anger again, warm and comforting.

"I have a life," she seethed. "I've moved on! You can't — You can't just—"

"Emma," he said. "Please. Just consider it!"

She shook her head, a hot tear spilling down her cheek. How dare he? How *dare* he barge back into her life, the life she'd convinced herself she was fine with, and see her so utterly?

"You think you can just charm your way into anything, huh?"

He laughed humorlessly. "Obviously not everything. Not the one person I actually—"

His muzzle snapped shut. He closed his eyes, the pain visible for a breathtaking millisecond before he closed himself off. His wings came down, shoulders relaxing.

When he smiled again, it was cool. Calm. Not oozing charm, but also no longer the cracked thing that had been there before.

"You're right," he said. "It was... it was ridiculous. Got caught up in the moment. I'm sorry."

His hand twitched. Like he'd been about to reach for her but forced himself to stop. Because he still knew her, after all this time. He knew she didn't like to be touched when she was like this. Didn't like being touched, period, unless it was someone she cared about.

"I'll go," he said quietly.

He turned. Emma watched him, eyes blurred with livid tears. Every part of her cried out to pull him back, scream in his face. To finally give him the telling-off that had been building in her chest for over a decade.

She grabbed his sleeve. He let out a surprised growl, letting her yank him around. He always did, even at the start. She'd been surprised: all that fur and muscle and he'd let a five-foot-nothing human tug him around like it was nothing. Then he kept letting her until he turned away from her that very last time. She'd reached for him and found him unmovable—like she was something he could shrug off on his way to his bright future.

And here he was. Standing there all contrite, eyes averted like they always were when he didn't want to have a conversation. But he didn't pull away.

"I hate you," Emma hissed.

Arthur winced. "Emma—"

She cut him off with a vicious kiss.

ELEVEN

She rode him into his plush carpet, teeth bared.

"Say it," she told him.

He stared up at her, claws digging into her hips. They still had their shirts on, barely managing to get her sweatpants off and his pants around his knees before she sat on his cock, so deep and fast it stung. He'd had to hold up her thighs, lowering her down until her pained gasps turned to sighs.

He was still staring, mouth hanging open to expose that beautiful pink tongue.

She worked her hips faster. "I said *say it*."

"I missed you," he said instantly. "Fuck, I missed you so much."

She thumbed her nipples, trying to find the furious-ness from before. Biting his lip as he carried her inside, shoving him down onto the carpet so hard he grunted. But he was so *huge* inside of her, hitting her sweet spot every time she moved, not to mention that face. Those big golden eyes kept ruining it. He gazed up at her so tenderly. Every time his eyes squeezed shut on some glorious flex of her hips, he forced them back open. Like he wanted to look at her as much as he could. Drinking her in to save for the drought later.

"Please," he gasped. "Shit, let me touch you."

She moaned, feeling him throb inside her. "You are touching me."

His big fingers flexed on her hips. "All of you. Please, I want it so bad. You're so beautiful."

Beautiful. He could've said hot or sexy or anything else, but he had to go with that sweet word.

She bit her lip. She kept telling herself this was going to be impersonal, angry, *rough*. But every part of her wanted to let her wrap him up in those stupid warm arms like he used to. Let him take care of her like he always did.

"Goddamnit," she panted. "Fine."

His hands were off her hips instantly. Sliding up her stomach, feeling the pouch that *definitely* wasn't there when she was nineteen, cupping her breasts with something that looked a lot like reverence. He touched her thighs, pocked with fresh claw marks. Then, like she knew he would, he ran his hands down her spine and sat up, burying his face in her neck. Holding her close.

Emma groaned into his mane as he started to take over, bouncing her in his lap. His hips moved in small, minute thrusts like he knew he wasn't supposed to but couldn't help himself. His thrusts grew stronger when she didn't tell him to lie back down and cut it out.

She was thinking about it. It just felt so damn *good* being surrounded by him again. Nobody held her like he did, tight and satisfying. Nobody *fucked* her like he did, impossibly huge and deep while he let out these helpless little growls against her cheek. He smelled like the expensive fur creams he'd brought along from LA, but underneath it was the scent she'd fallen asleep with for so much of high school. Just Arthur—stripped bare.

She stilled, letting him drive harder into her. She could feel the start of a knot at the base of his cock, just barely catching on her rim with each thrust.

"Knot me," she gasped.

His hips faltered. He pulled back, looking down at her. "You sure?"

She nodded fervently.

Arthur's golden eyes snapped shut, a groan forced between his fangs. He buried himself deep inside, holding her so tight it hurt.

She moaned helplessly. She'd *missed* this. Being crushed close, his arms shaking around her as his cock swelled. Tiny, jackrabbiting thrusts before his hips settled against her. He slumped, nuzzling her cheek.

"Emma," he whispered. "Emma."

She closed her eyes. She could feel his heartbeat matching hers, their ragged breathing coming in time. She'd forgotten what it felt like, being so close to someone you felt like you were one person.

Arthur kept muttering, the words mostly lost against her cheek. But not all of them: her name, of course. But also *can't believe* and *feels so good* and *missed you*.

Emma swallowed, trying to stop shaking. "Have you done this with anybody since me?"

She half expected him to scoff and tell her of course he had. The other half of her, the part that wasn't insecure and seething, expected nothing more than the incredulous laugh that rumbled through his chest.

"*Pfft*, sure. All knotting, all the time." He pulled back, his jokey smile going soft as he gazed up at her. "Come on, Emma. You think I'd let myself be like this in front of anyone else?"

Emma stared at him, stunned. She knew it, but there was a difference between knowing something and hearing someone say it.

Arthur's soft smile twitched, his ears flattening bashfully. "Uh, anyway. What about you?"

"Getting knotted?" Emma shook her head. "Nope. Just you."

"Oh," Arthur said quietly. "Good."

He swallowed. For a second, she thought he would take it back or ease the way with a joke. But he just lay there, his furry chest heaving and his swollen cock trapped inside of her.

"Good," he repeated before burying his face back in her neck.

"Huh," he muttered a while later.

She made a sleepy noise into his chest. "What?"

He nodded toward the giant window. "It's snowing again."

Emma turned. The snow was soft and silent, coating the white ground outside. Beyond the glass, Claw Haven glittered in the evening light.

Arthur ran a hand through her sweaty hair. "I wasn't going to sleep with you, you know. When I invited you on that tour. I wanted to talk. To make things right."

Good luck, Emma didn't say. There was still that sting of betrayal, but it was harder to find amongst the wash of endorphins. Emma wanted to believe him. To believe the way he'd looked at her while she was riding him, the way he was still looking at her now. His eyelids drooping, still trying to force himself to stay awake. Wanting to look at her a little longer.

Emma sighed. "You did love me, right? Back then. It was real."

Arthur's arms tightened around her, wings flexing like they wanted to follow suit. "Of course it was real. Why would you ask that?"

Emma shrugged.

Arthur laughed, thin and flinty. "Was I *that* bad of a boyfriend?"

"No," Emma admitted. "You just— You *left*."

She grimaced. It came out just as whiny and high school as she feared. That teenage bullshit she'd been running from was still there, she'd just grown around it.

Arthur sighed. "Come on, Emma. I had to follow my—"

"Heart?" Emma propped her chin up against his furry chest.

"Dreams," he corrected. He ran a hand down her

back, pressing his trimmed claws into the faint dents he'd left in her skin.

Emma tried not to think about how fast they would fade. "Is it everything you wanted? Being an actor?"

"Acting is great," Arthur said. He grinned, eyes creasing. "You know me, I'm an attention whore. The riches aren't bad, either. Or the awards. The travel, the cities. I really think you'd like LA if you gave it a chance."

Emma snorted, remembering that city. The trash, the dumb stores, the weird fashion, and the crowds she still had nightmares about.

"I did give it a chance, remember? Weeks of chances. I hate that place and it hates me."

"Emma. Come on—"

"My home is here," she insisted, staring out the glass at Claw Haven gleaming below. It looked so small from up here. There were no towering monuments, no glamor. The crowds were condensed into one tiny street. She'd grown up here. She never wanted to leave.

"I love it here," she said. "I know you think it's boring, even with the updates. But I just... I *love* it. It's part of me. Even when there's nowhere to get food after 10 p.m., and it doesn't get many movies, and there are no museums. I like the people, even if they piss me off almost as much as the tourists. I wake up every morning and I walk through the streets I've been walking down my whole life and I look over at the mountains, and the ocean, and the forest, and I feel... I don't know. Like I belong. Like I'm at peace."

Arthur was quiet. Emma looked up and found him

gazing out the window with her, his expression unreadable.

She dragged her fingers through his chest fur. "Is it peaceful in LA?"

"No," he replied. She expected him to shoot her a rakish grin and say that was what he liked about it. Finally, a place big enough for Arthur Pineclaw. But he just lay there, stroking her naked back absentmindedly, staring out over their hometown.

"I did miss you," he said finally. "There hasn't been anyone else like you."

"I bet not," she said flatly. She propped herself up on her elbows, clasping her hands under her chin like Luna had done to her at the cafe days ago. "*Oh Mr. Pineclaw, you're so dreamy! Can I get a photo? Can I touch your mane? You're soooo amazing.*"

"Alright, they're not *all* like that," he said, jostling her. "Seriously, though. Nobody takes me to task like you. Maybe I—"

His phone rang in his pocket, his jeans still stuck halfway down his thighs.

They stared at each other.

"I can ignore it," Arthur said quickly.

"No, no. Might be something important, Mr. Bigshot. I need to shower anyway." Emma shifted, testing the knot. It wasn't gone, but it had gone down enough for her to slip out. She eased herself off gently, both of them wincing as the widest part slid out of her with a slick pop.

· · ·

He was still on the phone when she headed out of the bathroom, half-dressed, toweling her hair dry. She could hear his voice from the hallway.

"No," he was saying as he paced the kitchen. He sounded like he was throwing something in the air— maybe an orange, he always used to mess around with the fruit bowl when he was bored as a teenager.

"Tell them no comment, then," he said. There was a pause. "*Everybody* says 'no comment' sometimes. Just because I have a good relationship with a lot of those vultures doesn't mean I owe them a quote."

Another pause. Arthur let out a very un-Arthur-like sigh before his tone went back to light and confident. "Fine. Tell them she's a wonderful costar, and we have fun together on and off set."

Emma's grip tightened on the towel in her hair. *Fun together on and off set*. She knew what she would assume if she read that in a gossip magazine. What was Arthur saying?

"They can take it however they want!" Arthur laughed. Then he paused, the laughter leaving his voice. "Right, uh. No. Emma was... we happened a million years ago. Ancient history. I'll be back in LA by Christmas. And good luck to anyone who tries to harass her, she'll chew them *right* out."

Somebody said something on the other end of the line. Arthur laughed again, and the noise only made the fire building in Emma's veins burn hotter.

Ancient history. I'll be back in LA by Christmas. Jennifer is fun on and off set. What kind of idiot was she, thinking she actually *mattered* to him? Even if he really hadn't knotted anybody else but her, even if she was the only person who ever saw him vulnerable. That wasn't enough for him to stay.

Emma charged into the kitchen dressed in only her underwear, a damp towel hanging from her hand.

"Gotta go, talk later." Arthur beamed, dropping his phone on the counter. He was dressed in a pair of boxers and nothing else, tossing an orange up in the air and catching it easily in one large hand. "Hey, you. My turn?"

Emma glared at him. "Who was that?"

Arthur blinked, surprised at the venom in her tone. Then his smile slid back into place, picture-perfect as always. "My agent. She asked if I wanted to comment on some photos that are going up. I told them that if they bothered you, you'd make them regret it."

"Bother me?"

Arthur hesitated, the orange coming to one last thud in his hand before he placed it back in the fruit bowl. "They have some photos of us kissing."

"But that just *happened*," she protested.

"Age of the iPhone." He scratched his mane guiltily. Her sweat was still drying in his fur, forming stiff peaks for him to rake his claws through.

"I'll keep your name out of the articles. People will still be able to find out who you are if they dig, but—"

Emma cut him off. "That must be bad publicity, with everything that's going on with Jennifer."

"Oh good, so you did hear that." Arthur sighed.

"Nothing is going on with Jennifer. I don't date coworkers until after shooting wraps."

"Do you sleep with them?"

"I haven't slept with her. Why? Are you worried?" Arthur grinned, fangs flashing in the dim room. It was so close to how he looked in all those movie posters that Emma felt sick.

"Emma," Arthur continued. He reached out to touch her bare waist.

Emma wrenched back, teeth clenched, stomach still roiling. She didn't want to feel *sick*. She wanted anger, hot and cleansing as it reached boiling point.

"Why would I be worried?" she snapped. "We're not together. We're not anything. God, why am I even here right now?"

She turned to leave. He leaped in front of her, hands raised pointedly.

"Because we're having a nice time!" he said, and the desperation in his voice made her pause. His eyes were huge and oddly pleading as he lowered his hands and placed them—slowly, cautiously—on her underwear-clad hips.

"I'm going to take a shower," he said. "Then we can... I don't know. Watch a movie. Order dessert. I can make a cafe fly something up. Or we can go down and continue the tour! There are stores that aren't on Main Street for me to mislabel, right?"

"Arthur," Emma said, teeth gritted.

He kissed her forehead. "Stay there. It'll be great, I promise! Night's far from over."

"*Arthur*," she snapped.

"Gonna be great," he repeated, already walking toward the bathroom, leaving Emma alone and mostly naked in the kitchen, shaking with rage.

I'll be back in LA by Christmas.

She knew. She *knew*, so why was she so angry? She'd been telling herself that since she arrived. But somehow, hearing him say it in that careless, flippant tone after he'd begged her to come and visit—after he'd stared at her so desperately while she rode him and held her so tightly—made her want to run into that bathroom. Scream in his face. But before she could take a step, his words from their first not-date flew through her head: *You feel something you don't like, and then you get mad. Because it's easier than feeling whatever's under it.*

"Fuck you," Emma whispered.

But there was a nagging truth to it, something cold and uncomfortable to match her boiling rage.

Emma breathed out shakily. For the first time, she looked under her anger. It took a while, standing there with her fists clenched in the kitchen. But as she peeled back those hot, satisfying layers, she noticed there were a dozen things under it. Betrayal, sadness, a mourning she'd been repressing for over a decade. And more than anything: exhaustion. She was so damn *tired*. She wanted to go back to normal. Having him for two weeks hurt more than never having him again.

Emma wiped her burning eyes. Then she crept into the living room, pulling on her crumpled clothes and shoes and hoping the shower would drown out the sound of the front door sliding open and closed.

She trudged toward the snowy path that led down the hill. Then she dug her phone out and dialed Luna's number.

Luna answered after two rings. "Well, hi there! If this is about dropping in on the book club, it just ended. But we're at Creature Comforts, they stayed open for us!"

"Great," Emma croaked, feeling like an idiot. "Um, I wanted to say sorry. For snapping at you the other day. You were just trying to help."

"Aw, that's fine. I shouldn't have pried, but you know I love gossip." Luna paused. "Are you alright? You sound... different."

Emma bit her tongue, fighting the urge to tell Luna to mind her fucking business. Never mind that she called her. Never mind that she would have to slog down the mountain in a ratty pair of sneakers and not enough layers. Then Arthur's voice came to her once again: *You have to open up, not just hide under the anger.*

Goddamnit, Emma thought. *I might actually have to thank the bastard.*

"Actually, I'm not doing so great," she admitted in a rush. "Can you pick me up?"

TWELVE

Emma was gone.

No goodbye. Not even a wave. Just a conspicuously empty cabin and a text message he found when he was considering calling the cops to report a kidnapping.

Got a ride home, the text message said.

Arthur had stood there in the living room for a long time, staring at the screen and trying to convince himself there wasn't a pit opening in his chest. Even with that last-minute argument, he thought they were getting along. He had been more vulnerable with her in the past week and a half than he had been with anybody in the last *decade*. Not to mention the knotting, which had made him feel like a fumbling teenager all over again. Or, more accurately, it made him feel something he hadn't felt since he was a teenager. Stripped bare, nothing to hide. Just Arthur.

She didn't message him again. Not when he asked if she wanted to get coffee the next day or dinner the day after that. Not until he asked if she'd seen the articles that had just come out, full of hazy half-truths about their teenage relationship and damning photos of them mid-kiss, her fingers tangled in his mane.

I really did try to get them to pull those stories, he messaged her. *I know you like your privacy.*

This, finally, was what made her break her silence. He opened the message expecting anger, annoyance, or at least wary exasperation.

Her reply had none of that. It was one sentence, short and bland enough to make him wish she had called him up to yell at him.

Thanks for trying.

Jennifer ambushed him several days later as a makeup artist rearranged his mane.

"This is ridiculous," she said, tugging a blanket tighter around her and shivering. "Give me a soundstage and potato flakes any day. I'm freezing my toes off."

"You get used to it," he assured her. He sent her a reassuring smile, staying as still as possible for the makeup artist tugging at his mane. They were standing in the middle of Main Street, filming the confession scene.

Jennifer stood next to him, watching Rusty tell off the camera crew. Somebody had dropped an important piece of sound equipment, and they were running out of time. They only had a few hours before the sun started going down.

"I thought you'd gotten warm blood in LA," Jennifer said. "The cold definitely seems to be affecting you now."

"Is it?"

She laughed. "You've flubbed more lines today than you have in this whole shoot! You can admit your mane isn't *that* thick. I know some chimeras back home, and they can't even cope with frost."

Arthur forced a laugh. He'd botched more than a few lines because he was too busy watching the street they were shooting on, hoping Emma would walk by. They'd closed it off, but there were still people gathered around the barriers, taking photos or asking for autographs in between takes. Arthur had been over to them a few times before Rusty made him stop.

"You ferreted me out," Arthur said. "I can't deal with Alaskan winters anymore."

Jennifer beamed. "I knew it."

The makeup artist gave his mane one last painful comb and then raced off. Jennifer swayed sideways, her blanketed elbow brushing his.

"Sooo," she said. "Talked to Rusty lately?"

Arthur gave her a blank look. They had all been talking to Rusty. He was the director, and they'd talked to him five minutes ago.

"Alone," she explained.

"Not today," he said. "Why? Am I getting fired?"

She laughed, shoulders shaking with it. She even

squeezed his bicep, which made him nervous. *Was* he getting fired, or was she just flirting? She didn't usually lay it on this thick. Especially not when anyone was in earshot. She usually waited for some of the crew to come close. It was her way of keeping the gossip rags fed, Randy told him before shooting started back in LA. She made it look like an accident, but she never let anything slip that she didn't discuss with her agent first.

"Nobody's going to fire Arthur Pineclaw," she said. "Seriously, though. You should talk to him later."

A dozen things ran through Arthur's head: another movie contract, a bizarre publicity stunt, a last-minute rewrite. Those articles about Emma coming back to bite him in the ass. *Movie star's surprise fling with ex-fiance while filming in hometown.* It was just bad reporting. They were never technically engaged. Even if he had been looking at rings before that fateful Christmas Eve.

"I'll see what I can do," he said and grinned.

He met Rusty at Sour Claw after shooting had ended for the day.

"What a fucking shoot," Rusty said, throwing back his second whiskey since they sat down. His face twisted up. "Shit. You did not joke about how crappy this stuff is. *This* is the best they can do?"

Arthur grunted in agreement, swishing it around in his mouth. He hated to admit it, but it was growing on him.

"It was the cold," he said as Rusty placed the glass down on the dirty bar with a disgusted look.

Rusty looked over. "Huh?"

"All the line flubs." Arthur winced, performative and handsome. He could do anything handsomely, including apologize. "I'll do better when we're out of the subzero temperatures."

"Right," Rusty said distractedly. "Sure."

Arthur stared into his glass. Emma would have poked holes in that excuse without a thought. Nobody ever poked holes in his excuses anymore. Which was good, for a long time. It was better that way. It was certainly easier when no one really knew what was going on with you. When you hardly even knew yourself, perfectly content to believe in the mask you showed everybody. Emma was always pulling back the damn mask, always *seeing* him.

Maybe that was what had happened. She'd seen him and decided he wasn't with it.

"Arthur. Arthur!"

Arthur jolted. He looked up to find Rusty waving his cap in front of his face expectantly.

"It is *not* cold enough for you to be spacey in here," Rusty announced, shoving his cap back on his balding head. "Hey. So. Wanted to talk to you about something, bud."

He inched his chair over. Arthur did the same, eyeing a fairy fluttering at the end of the bar with a dishcloth. She'd gotten Arthur to sign her boobs that first night, and she looked like she was going to do her damnedest to listen in before an elderly minotaur hobbled over and pointed toward a broken glass near the toilets.

The fairy fluttered toward where he was pointing, a broom in her hand.

Arthur turned back to Rusty, satisfied no one was going to spill their secrets to the closest tabloid. "What's up?"

"We think it'd be a good idea for you and Jen to start something before the movie comes out next year."

Arthur felt his tail flick behind him. He stilled it immediately. It wouldn't be the first time he'd been asked to start something up with a costar for publicity purposes. Sometimes it was just a few candids, other times it was a genuine relationship. It depended on how far they wanted to take it.

"Right," Arthur said, straightening his shirt collar. "Of course. Real or fake?"

"Whatever you want." Rusty took another slug of whiskey. "But between you and me, she's all for it. Really for it—and you'd have to be an idiot to turn *that* down."

Arthur laughed. It felt stale, but he was good at his job. Nobody would've been able to tell it was bullshit. Nobody except one human who wouldn't text him back.

"I'm totally with you," he said.

"Great." Rusty dug in his jeans pocket. "I'll let her know. And your agent, she helped me set it up, tell her I said thanks. Now—"

Arthur cut him off. "Actually, can we hold off on that?"

Rusty paused, fingers hovering over the screen. "On telling your agent?"

"On the whole thing." Arthur beamed, channeling every bit of charm he had into it. "I need to check on something first."

Irritation flickered over Rusty's tired face. Then he took a drink and it was replaced by a tight smile.

"Sure," he said. "Let me know by tomorrow, alright bud? We need to get photos before filming shuts down. Makeup chair shots, and you two eating together between takes, goofing off. All that fun shit. We'll have to say it started pretty late in the game since there are those photos of you and your ex making out. Have any paparazzi been bothering you?"

"No." Most of the photos that had ended up online, including the ones of him and Emma kissing during the tour, had been taken by opportunistic tourists. Claw Haven was a long way to travel for most paparazzi.

Rusty clapped his shoulder. "Glad to hear it, bud."

Arthur watched him finish off his glass. He'd heard Rusty talking to paparazzi on the phone earlier today, trying to make them come up to Claw Haven. Arthur wasn't mad—it was good for Rusty's career, for *both* their careers. But it made Arthur think back to that time Rusty had admitted he was surprised Arthur didn't like paparazzi since he got along with them so well.

I thought you thrived on the attention, Rusty had told him over his at-home bar. *Sure, they're pushy. But I thought you didn't care about that. Anything for a spotlight, or whatever.*

Arthur had smiled and laughed and said all the right things. But it had rankled him in some deep-down place he tried not to look at. *Anything for a spotlight.* Was that what people thought of him? Was that still what *Rusty* thought?

He watched Rusty texting away and tried to think of a conversation they'd had that didn't eventually circle back to work. He couldn't. Which was.... fine. Arthur liked talking about work. He enjoyed it. He didn't talk about personal stuff very much, anyway. Neither did Rusty. Actually, Arthur couldn't come up with much about Rusty's personal life. He had a wife, he didn't work out, he failed out of boarding school... and that was it.

Arthur's tail flicked again. He stilled it. It had been happening too much since he came to Claw Haven; he'd have to sort that out before he went back to LA. He couldn't walk around telegraphing what he was feeling all the time.

Was Rusty a friend or a coworker? Scratch that. Was everyone in Arthur's life—his agent, his LA flying crew, his gym instructor, the old coworkers he got brunch with every eight months that never ended without a photo op —were they *all* just coworkers? He couldn't think of a truly personal conversation he'd had with any of them. Nor with his parents. The only genuine connection he had was with Emma Curt.

He almost wanted to laugh. It would be better than bursting into tears, which was feeling horrifyingly like a real option as he sat there at the bar, ignored by his coworker, stared at by bar patrons and fairy waitresses who wanted an autograph, and ignored by the one person who truly saw him.

Arthur stood up so fast he nearly knocked over the barstool with his wings.

"I have to go," he announced.

Rusty watched him go, bewildered. "You're gonna get back to me about that thing we talked about, right?"

"On it," Arthur called back. He stumbled out of the bar, heart thumping, the future warping in front of him in a way it hadn't done in a long, long time.

He dug his blunt claws into his hands, tail twitching as he waited on her ramp. He should've brought flowers. He should've shown up at her house days ago, no matter what Joshua said about letting things lie. He should've done a lot of things.

The door creaked warily open, revealing Emma in all her sweatpants and sleep-shirt glory. Her hair was oily like it hadn't been washed in a few days, and she was wearing fuzzy socks as slippers. She was the most beautiful thing he had ever seen.

"They want me to date my costar," Arthur said, too loud. Then he stopped. "Is that my shirt?"

The door stopped. For a second, Arthur thought she would slam it in his face, or maybe take the wreath off the door and throw it at him. She seemed like she was considering it.

"I found it in my parents' garage a few years ago,"

Emma said slowly, like she had to force it out. "It's comfy."

"Looks comfy," Arthur said determinedly. "I mean, good. It looks really good on you."

Emma's lips tightened. Arthur braced himself for a snarky comment, Emma's go-to defense when she felt like the other person had the upper hand.

"I threw it in the trash," she admitted. "Then, um, dug it out. What were you saying about Jennifer?"

"Nothing is happening," Arthur hurried to say. "I swear. They just want me to date her for the publicity."

He glanced around, trying to spot any werewolves or vampires who might be lingering down the street with their super hearing. The street was empty, and he couldn't smell anyone hiding in the bushes. Just snow and Emma's berry deodorant buried under dried sweat. It made him want to follow her inside and lick it off of her. Wrap her in a blanket when they were done. He'd never seen the inside of her house, and he wanted to know how she lived. If she still organized her bookshelf by color, kept DVDs, or left the cupboard doors hanging open even though she always dinged her head on them. He knew her to her bones, but he didn't know what her bedroom looked like. He wanted to.

Emma waited. "And?"

"It would be fake," Arthur continued, forcing his thoughts back on track. "At least while we're in Claw Haven. Like I said, I don't date coworkers after shooting wraps. Maybe after. I wanted to run it by you first."

Emma's jaw ticked. She folded her arms, and his heart sank.

"Again, why would I care?" she asked.

He blinked. It actually sounded like a question this time, not the accusation she'd slung at him at the cabin.

"Because I thought we had something the other day. Before you ran out into the snow." Arthur could feel the desperation in his smile. He knew she could see it, she always could. And yet he couldn't stop. If he stopped, he didn't know what terrifyingly honest expression would take over his face, but he didn't want anyone to witness it.

"It had stopped snowing," Emma said defensively. She shifted from foot to foot, obviously uncomfortable. But not yelling. Why wasn't she yelling?

"We did have something," Emma admitted in a rush, staring at her socked feet. "But you're—you're leaving. So let's just stop whatever this is before one of us does something stupid."

He'd never seen her this quiet when she was upset. It was eerie. It made him want to take her face and tilt it up, make her look at him. He dug his claws into his hands, forcing them to still.

"You really aren't going to yell?" he asked hopefully.

She huffed. "I'm trying something new. I'm still mad, I'm just... I don't know. I'm trying to be done with yelling. I'm trying to be done with *this*."

She waved between them. Then she added something he didn't expect.

"I'm sorry," she said.

She started closing the door.

Arthur panicked, shoving his wing in the way.

"I wanted you to come with me," he tried. "I thought about you all the time; I tried not to, but I did. You can still come with me!"

Emma snorted, his old shirt falling off her shoulder and exposing her collarbone in a way that made him breathless.

"Right," she said. "I'm going to be the next girl on your arm, huh? All prettied up and smiling, going to parties and red carpets and laughing at everyone's jokes. That's who I'm gonna be?"

"You can fake it," he said. "It's not that hard! I can teach you!"

Emma nudged his wing out of the way, so gently he was too dumbfounded to do anything but let her.

He grabbed the door. "Please! I need— Nobody's ever— *Please*."

Emma finally met his gaze. Her beautiful brown eyes were shining, goosebumps already rising on the exposed flesh of her shoulder. She sucked in a deep breath like he'd always told her to do when they were in high school, one bit of advice she had never followed. She'd always steamrollered ahead, not taking the time to pause and cool down before she started screaming.

Except now. She'd finally started doing it. It just took him breaking her heart for a second time.

"We had something good," she said, her voice almost even. "And it ended. And that's... fine. It's fine! I've moved on. You've moved on. And now we go back to our lives."

She paused and smiled at him, small and tremulous.

"I'm glad you came back to visit," she admitted quietly. "Merry Christmas, Arthur."

She closed the door. No slamming, no screaming. Just a soft *snick* of the lock clicking into place and the not-so-soft sound of Arthur trying to stop the heart-broken roar building in his throat.

THIRTEEN

Emma avoided the cafe during the last day of the shoot.

In her defense, she had shit to organize. Social media posts to queue up for the Instagram account Luna insisted on her making, which would tell everyone that normal business hours would resume the day after Christmas. Last-minute presents to buy for her employees. A tree to put up. And most importantly, a wrap party to emotionally prepare for.

Luna called her as she was wrapping presents. "Hey Em! You still coming? Everything's all set up at the inn, and it's party time! Christmas Eve party and wrap party all in oneeee!"

Emma propped the phone up on a roll of wrapping paper and went back to badly wrapping a mug she'd gotten for Hazel.

"I'll be late," she warned. "I have a call with my parents, and we're putting up a tree."

Luna cooed. "Aw! Cute! We love a family call at Christmas. How are you feeling?"

Emma bit her cheek. Her knee-jerk response was to change the subject. But she was earnestly trying this whole *opening up* crap, and Luna had been good about it. Hadn't made fun of her once.

"I've been better," Emma said warily. "I'm getting a punching bag. Late Christmas present to myself. It'll be here by New Year."

"Yay!" Luna said. "I'm so proud of you. It's hard telling people what's really going on. God knows I suck at it! Anyway, see you at the party. I'll save you some eggnog."

Emma barely had time to hang up before a video call came in.

Her parents' faces flickered into view, both of them leaning in so close to the screen she could see their pores. They both looked exhausted but happy, and Emma's heart clenched.

"Hi," they chorused in one.

Emma waved. "Hey! One second, I have this one last thing to wrap."

She eased another raggedy piece of wrapping paper over the mug. It was shoddily done, but she doubted Hazel would mind. She placed it to the side and shuffled over to the plastic Christmas tree they'd bought her when she first moved out.

"Okay," she said, slapping the box of decorations she'd dragged out from the garage. "Ready. Where's yours?"

Glen held up a tiny plastic tree they must've bought at a gift shop the last time they docked. It was barely the size of his forearm.

"We had trouble finding decorations small enough," Bitsey explained. "But we have some!"

There was a pause as they both arranged their cameras in front of their trees. Emma strung tinsel around her tree, grinning as she listened to her parents squabble over the proper way to hang a car air freshener on their minuscule tree. Apparently, the air freshener was one of the only decorations they could find that was small enough, as well as a Santa head bauble, a mini candy cane, and pipe cleaners instead of tinsel.

"I love it," Bitsey declared. "I think this might be our best tree ever."

Emma laughed. "Hello?"

"Yours is okay, I guess," Bitsey amended, leaning into the frame to see it. "Oh, that's lovely. Glen, look, she put up that one she made in grade school. I thought you'd thrown it out."

"I thought about it," Emma said. "But... I don't know. Seemed like the time to bring it back out. Been thinking a lot about the past recently."

Bitsey traded a look with Glen, who abruptly appeared in the frame.

"We were just talking about that last Christmas we spent together," Glen admitted. "Us and Arthur, I mean. We'd just finished the tree, then Arthur took you on a walk. Then you came back and he was gone."

Emma gritted her teeth. She didn't want to do this

right before she had to go to the party and see him schmoozing with his costar who he may or may not be dating. Especially if he was going to try to talk to her again, all sad and vulnerable like last time. Of course, he'd finally let his mask drop when it was too late.

"We were so surprised," Glen continued. "We really thought you two kids were going to last."

Emma cut him off. "Yeah, can we not talk about that? Bit of a buzzkill."

"Oh." Glen paused. "Sorry. You made all that noise about talking more about, um, your feelings—"

"But we won't talk about it if you don't want to," Bitsey said, fixing Glen with another pointed look. She readjusted the phone, the camera swinging to see the cabin carpet and the ceiling before focusing again on their faces.

"Great," Emma said, shoulders sagging. "So, how are things on the boat?"

"He did call me a few years ago," Bitsey added. "Asked how you were doing."

Glen gave her a look that clearly meant, *why am I not allowed to talk about it, but you are?* But he didn't look surprised. How long had they been sitting on this?

Emma swallowed. "What do you mean? He never called."

"He did," Bitsey said. "This was New Year's morning... what was it, five years back?"

"Four," Glen corrected.

"Four or five," Bitsey said. "He was *very* drunk. He said he was dating a lot, and that they were fun, but you were the only real thing in his life. The only person who really loved him."

"*Why*—?" Emma forced her voice to lower. "Why didn't you tell me?"

"He begged us not to. And then when we *did* try to tell you, you yelled at us."

Emma grimaced. "Yeah, that—that sounds like me."

She sat down on the carpet, mind reeling. Four or five *years* ago. She'd had no idea. She thought about his desperate expression the last time he came to her house, his wing stopping the door from closing.

Please, he'd said, voice rawer than she'd ever heard it. *I need— Please.*

"He said he missed us, too," Bitsey continued. "Me and your father. It was very sweet. He even started crying."

Emma laughed shakily. "Are you sure? He never cries. I'm surprised he can squeeze out a tear for a movie."

"Well, he did." Bitsey reached out of the screen, coming back with the tiny Christmas tree and holding it between her and Glen. "Anyway, how are you doing? Are you going to that party?"

Emma swallowed. She couldn't stop imagining Arthur in an empty mansion on New Year's morning, maybe slumped in a bathtub, maybe on a bed, tears rolling into his fur. Why the hell didn't he call *her*? Would she have picked up? She liked to think she would, even just to yell at him for daring to do it.

"Emma?"

"Yeah," Emma said, voice only wavering a little bit. "I'm—I'm gonna go."

"Oh, good," Glen said. Then, after yet another pointed look from Bitsey, "And how are you feeling about that?"

"Fine," Emma said. Then she sighed. "I mean. Not fine. But I'm not dreading it. I just need to get through tonight."

One more night with this strange new version of Arthur at arm's reach. Then he'd go back to his life, and she'd go back to hers. And neither of them was going to do anything stupid to jeopardize that.

Luna emerged through the crowded common room with a warm mug of eggnog. It was topped with melting whipped cream and chocolate flakes.

She pushed it into Emma's hands and leaned in to yell over the din. "Told you I'd save you some! Are you a hugger yet?"

Emma held the mug in front of her like a shield. "I said I was being more open. I didn't say I was turning into a hugger. The two aren't mutually exclusive."

"Fine by me," Luna said, flicking her blonde hair over her shoulder and almost hitting a human Emma recognized as part of the camera crew. There was a bunch of the crew scattered around, mostly keeping to their groups while all the extras stood in their own clumps. The extras hadn't originally been invited, but apparently, Luna had pulled some strings.

Luna gave her a friendly shoulder pat instead. "You're coming to dinner tomorrow, right? We'd love to have you."

Emma pictured a table full of the Musgrove family, with all their yelling and laughing and teasing. It sounded nice, if a little overwhelming.

"I'm not great with big groups," she admitted. "But I'll definitely drop by. Thanks again for the invite."

"Of course!" Luna twisted to look through the crowd. "I'm going to go see my husband. The nephews talked him into a contest to see who he could throw the farthest, and I have bets to cash in on. You'll be okay if I dash off?"

Emma nodded, clutching her eggnog and reminding herself that she only had to stay for ten minutes. If she still wasn't feeling it, she could go home. Out of this damn crowd and away from the danger zone of possibly running into Arthur.

"Toodles!" Luna started weaving through the crowd.

Emma sipped her eggnog and almost choked. The sweetness was almost completely overpowered by the liquor.

"Pretty intense," said a voice next to her.

Emma turned. Daisy was squeezing between makeup artists to stand at her side, tugging Hazel behind her.

"I couldn't finish mine," Daisy continued, ears twitching like they sometimes did when she was stuck somewhere very loud. "If I wanted something that strong, I'd drink shots. Hazel's loving it, though."

Hazel let out a whoop. She was swaying to the music, her elbows and hips knocking into anyone unfortunate enough to be standing close, which happened to include Daisy and Emma.

"Oops," Hazel said, lowering her arms. "Sorry, boss. And Daisy."

She took another slug from her eggnog, which was almost gone. *Almost* being the key word as it slipped from Hazel's clumsy grip and clattered to the carpet, spilling over all their shoes.

"Oops," Hazel repeated, dropping to her knees. She grabbed at the whipped cream, grimacing as it smeared over her fingers. "Crap!"

"Daisy," Emma began.

"Already on it," Daisy said, pushing through the party toward the kitchen for cleanup fodder.

Emma examined her boots, now stained with snow *and* eggnog. That old irritation flared up again, mixing with the stress of tonight and not enough alcohol. It was obvious enough to show on her face because Hazel only looked more nervous when she glanced up.

"I got it," she said unconvincingly, dabbing uselessly at Emma's boots and smearing whipped cream into the leather. "Crap. I'm *so* sorry."

Emma entertained a brief fantasy of yelling at her. Maybe it would make people finally stop pressing all around her and give her some air. It would be so satisfying, unleashing her anxiety on Hazel, who had pissed her off so much already.

Emma took a deep breath and squatted down. "I haven't been that nice to you."

Hazel paused. She was in the middle of slopping some of the carpet cream back into the mug, with mixed results.

"You're alright," Hazel said, fast and a little frightened.

"I'm an asshole," Emma replied. "I know how hard it is, starting a new job. And even if it's not coming naturally to you, I see how hard you try. You try harder than any of us. So... thank you. For that."

Hazel blinked hard, eyes bright in the dim party light. "I swear I'll be better soon. It's my New Year's resolution! No customer complaints about how bad my coffees are."

"Let's aim a little lower," Emma told her.

Microphone feedback screeched around the room. Emma and Hazel flinched, a few monsters letting out a pained cry as their sensitive ears were assaulted.

"Sorry," came Rusty's not-so-apologetic voice. "Sorry, everybody. If we could get everyone toward the back of the room, we have a few words from our stars."

Emma's stomach dropped. She took another hopeful mouthful of her eggnog, then decided it wasn't worth it. Shots would be a hundred times better than this sickeningly sweet swill.

She turned to find Arthur and Jennifer standing queasily close, leaning over the shared microphone.

"We just wanted to say thank you for your hard work," Arthur began. "You guys were fantastic. Can't wait to see this in theaters next Christmas. Jen?"

He tilted the microphone. In the background, Rusty darted around taking pictures on his phone. He motioned at Jennifer, who smiled even wider. She even managed to make it look natural.

"I had reservations about the wig," she admitted, with a resounding laugh from the makeup team. "But you guys made it work!"

She slipped her hand into Arthur's. "I looked good, right?"

Arthur laughed. They suited each other, Emma realized resentfully. That specific brand of Hollywood perfect, teeth too straight and hair too shiny, completely relaxed with all eyes on them. Except for that barely-there tightness around Arthur's eyes, betraying his discomfort.

"You looked amazing," he said. He turned toward the crowd. "I wanted to thank Claw Haven for letting us show off their home for this movie."

"Your home too," came a shout from the crowd. It sounded a lot like Jasper Dawn, that annoying vampire who worked at the hospital.

Jennifer nudged him. "Was it good to be back?"

Arthur cleared his throat. "It was great. It was... it was *really* great, being back. I—"

He stopped, his smile freezing as he noticed Emma through the crowd.

Emma's stomach twisted. She'd never seen him lost for words before. Jennifer eyed him curiously, Rusty pausing in his picture-taking to shoot him a pointed look.

Arthur didn't seem to notice.

"I—" he repeated. His hand flexed around Jennifer's, his smile solidifying as he addressed the crowd once again. "Anyway! Great job, everyone. Enjoy the free booze. I gotta..."

He trailed off, uncharacteristically uncharismatic as he detangled himself from Jennifer and headed into the crowd to a chorus of clapping and an enthusiastic whoop from Hazel, who was busy getting wiped clean with Daisy's napkins.

"We should go," Daisy told Hazel, ears flicking nervously as she looked over at Emma. "Right?"

She was asking if Emma needed backup for this inevitable interaction. Emma thought about telling them to stay. Then she made the stupid decision of looking at Arthur again, his gaze intent on her as he made his way through the crowd. A few people tried to talk to him, but he gave them a distracted grin and kept going.

"Yep," Emma croaked.

Daisy pulled Hazel away, still wiping eggnog cream off her hands.

Arthur stopped in front of her, somehow managing to look small despite his height, mane, and giant shoulders.

"Emma," he said. "You came! I heard you couldn't make it."

"I'm only here for a while," Emma said, searching desperately for a lie. "I, uh, have a headache."

"Oh." Arthur twisted toward the kitchen. "I can get you something."

"No, no!" She caught his arm before he could go running off. "It's fine. I have eggnog."

He looked down at her hand. She dropped it, skin tingling with the feel of the sleek fabric. She missed the anger. The first few times she'd seen him in town, her fury had been so big it blotted everything out. Now all the emotions she'd been suppressing were flooding to the surface. Standing in front of him felt like an exercise in yearning, every inch of her wanting to take his arm again. Step closer. Run her fingers through the fur over his cheeks, tug him down in front of everybody.

"I thought you'd be on the phone with your parents," Arthur said, jolting her out of her useless daydream. "Setting up the Christmas tree."

"Already done." Emma smiled, trying and failing not to think about her mother's matter-of-fact voice as she told her that Arthur had cried. She couldn't help but picture him in his mid-twenties, alone in what would have to be a mansion by that point. His tears rolling down his furry cheeks as he sat in the remains of a New Year's party, mumbling down the phone to his ex-girl-friend's parents.

"What about you?" Emma asked. "Any Christmas traditions?"

Arthur shrugged. "Not really. Any that I had, I had because of you."

Emma's traitorous heart spasmed in her chest. Before she could say anything to that, Hazel came squeezing through the crowd. Other than specks of cream on her shirt, she was completely clean.

"I'm not interrupting," she insisted. "I'm just leaving, and I have to say goodbye first. Bye! And Merry Christmas!"

"Merry Christmas," Emma replied, thankful for the interruption from Arthur's big, sad, golden eyes. "I'll drop off your gift tomorrow."

Hazel clasped her cream-streaked chest. "That's so nice. *Thank* you. I really will try harder next year."

"You try hard enough already," Emma assured her. "I really appreciate it."

Daisy appeared at Hazel's shoulder, tugging gently. Hazel let her drag her away, both of them waving as they vanished into the crowd.

"That was sweet," Arthur said. "She didn't seem scared of you at all."

Emma sighed. "Probably because I apologized for being a hardass. Explained some stuff. I'm trying that whole... *open* thing."

"That's great!" Arthur said, so loud that several people looked over. He coughed, lowering his voice. "That's really great, Emma."

There was an annoyed little voice inside her telling her she was being patronized. But it was hard to believe when he was looking at her like this, his tail swishing and then stilling, then swishing again, like he had to continuously remind himself to cut it out.

Emma closed her eyes. She needed to make an exit soon before she did something stupid.

"So," she said. "Flying out soon?"

"Tonight. After this."

"Excited to get home?"

Arthur didn't reply. He was still staring at her, his distracted smile getting smaller and smaller until his face was all desperation.

He stepped closer, so close that she could hear his intake of breath over the din. The world fell away. The uncomfortable press of the crowd, the laughter and conversation, and the dreaded warmth of everyone's bodies filling the same space narrowed down into Arthur standing in front of her, gazing down at her like he'd never wanted anything else.

Which, of course, was a lie. But he made it hard to remember that. Made it hard to think about anything but how good he would feel pressed against her, holding her close.

"Emma," Arthur began. "I—"

His next word was cut off as Rusty appeared at his side, waving his phone.

"Arthur!" he said, cheeks red with excitement and eggnog. "Come and get a photo. Your lady awaits."

That was Emma's cue.

"I'm going to go," she said, turning toward the doorway.

Arthur made a lost sound in the back of his throat. Half-growl, half-whimper. She'd never heard it before.

"Wait," he said.

"Have a good flight, Arthur." Emma squeezed through the crowd. She didn't look back until she was at the doorway.

Arthur was standing with Jennifer, his arm around

her waist. She was leaning into him, giggling at something Rusty was saying as he aimed his phone camera at them. She said something to Arthur, who nodded.

He was smiling. He looked perfectly normal if you didn't know what to look for.

But Emma did. She saw it all: the spasming tail he kept trying to still, those beautiful laugh lines turning hard before he forced them to soften.

Emma swallowed. She'd been an idiot to think he had been unaffected by their breakup. She'd bought into his bullshit for once, too blinded by anger to look past it.

The camera light flashed. Arthur's smile widened, strained.

I might never see him again, Emma thought.

Then she left, resolutely ignoring her heart as it cracked open in her chest.

FOURTEEN

Everyone at the goddamn party wanted to say goodbye to Arthur before they left.

Arthur stuck it out. Smiled through every handshake and photo and autograph until Musgrove Inn was almost empty and it was time to go.

"The photo's doing rounds on socials," Rusty told him as he finished his last eggnog. "Everybody's speculating about you two. I know I tell you this all the time, but you're the *best* when it comes to looking at your leading lady."

"Thanks," Arthur said, making sure his voice was extra peppy to make up for the deep pit that had formed in him when he had watched Emma leave. Was this how she felt, watching him walk off after their last Christmas walk? Especially after the crap that he'd said to her about holding him back. She hadn't even raised her voice. If he felt this shitty when she'd left him on okay terms, he couldn't imagine how she had felt all those years ago.

Rusty was still talking. Arthur tuned in just in time to hear him say, "If they gave out awards for this shit, you'd get the gold. Hey, before we head off, I wanted to ask you something."

Arthur tore his eyes away from the door, where the last party stragglers were heading off with their Arthur autographs and mourning that they hadn't been able to catch Jennifer before she ducked out. She was on a flight tomorrow morning, and she wanted to be rested for it.

"Shoot," Arthur said.

Rusty pointed at him. His cheeks were ruddy, his cap was twisted backward for the third time tonight, and his hair was a mess underneath it. He had the slightest slur to betray how much eggnog he'd had.

"I'm not meant to be telling you about this yet," he said. "But I'm gonna anyway. I signed up to shoot another rom-com, and I want you in on it. It's fake dating; everybody's frothing at the mouth for that. You'd be in New York for four months. What do you say?"

Arthur hesitated. Two weeks ago, he would've said yes. Would've said *hell* yes. He liked working with Rusty, he liked doing rom-coms, and his agent would be happy with him, even if it wasn't the dramatic roles she'd been pushing him toward. New York would be another fun city in a string of fun locations he was shooting in, film after film, year after year. A constant string of parties and lights and noise, people all around, gushing at him, squeezing his biceps, asking for photos. Watching him on big screens and streaming sites and billboards. Everyone looking at him, but no one seeing him.

"Arthur," Rusty said. "Hey. You in there?"

"What? Of course." Arthur felt his tail swish and stilled it with a sigh. If Emma could start opening up, then so could he. "I'm just... I'm not really myself tonight."

"Oh." Rusty scratched his stubble. "Really? What's up?"

Arthur tried not to be disappointed that Rusty didn't notice. He had tried to hide it, after all. It was good that nobody had caught on.

"Just... ex crap," he finished lamely and winced. It sounded cheap to describe it like that. But he didn't want to go into it, especially when Rusty was looking at him all glazed and distracted, ready to get in the car and head to the airport.

"Never mind," Arthur continued. "Look, thanks for the offer. Can I get back to you after Christmas?"

"Sure." Rusty downed the last of his eggnog and slammed the glass onto the drinks table. "Come on, car's waiting. You have your stuff from the cabin, right?"

"It's behind the counter."

Rusty smacked him on the back. "Great! Let's go."

Arthur watched him swagger into the lobby beside him and realized what he'd been waiting for. He'd assumed Rusty would be annoyed, the way he always was when Arthur didn't do what he wanted.

Rusty peeled off toward the front doors with a jaunty wave. Arthur returned it, wondering what Rusty would do if he stopped him and told him everything that had happened over the past two weeks. Trying to make things right and then falling head over heels into feelings he thought he'd left behind over a decade ago. Watching Emma finally start to open up to the people around her, his pride mixed with a strange panic that he wouldn't be around to see it.

He had a sneaking suspicion that Rusty wouldn't give a shit. Just like at Sour Claw. He'd pretended, sure. But he wasn't a good actor. Arthur had been giving him the benefit of the doubt for too long.

He headed for the counter, pausing when he spotted a familiar minotaur straightening a wreath that hung off the till.

"Oh, hello," said Joshua Haberdash, tweaking a sprig of holly. "I thought you'd left."

"I'm on my way. Car's out front." Arthur stooped behind the counter and picked up his suitcase. "Merry Christmas."

"You too." Joshua smiled, wiping that infuriatingly dry fur out of his eyes. "It was good to see you. You should come back and visit when the movie comes out."

"Right," Arthur said. "Good publicity."

"Sure," Joshua said. "Also, we'd love to see you."

He was as buttoned-up as ever, with no spills or even sweat on his clothes. He didn't smell like eggnog, just the usual flowery scent that followed him around his day job. He straightened the wreath again. It kept listing to the side. Joshua huffed in irritation, flicking fur out of his eyes once more.

Arthur was struck by a sudden inspiration. He set his

suitcase down, unzipping the front pocket and pulling out a small, shiny tube.

He held it out. "It's not wrapped, but Merry Christmas."

Joshua looked up from the wreath. "Oh! Um."

"It's fur cream," Arthur explained. "From the best specialist in LA. It'll fix the dryness. Make it glossy. Give you more volume. Less flopping in your eyes."

He gestured at the dull fur hanging over Joshua's face. Joshua flicked it out of the way self-consciously and took the tube. For a moment, Arthur thought he'd fucked up and insulted his dry fur, but after another second of shock, Joshua broke out into a shy grin.

"Wow," he said. "I've heard of this brand. This is *fancy*. Thank you, that's so nice."

"Yeah. Well." Arthur grabbed his suitcase and headed for the front doors. "Wanted to return the favor, Haber-dash. Those white tulips worked wonders."

Joshua's grin faded into something softer. "Good. You guys were always really great for each other."

Arthur slowed, a wave of exhaustion washing over him that had nothing to do with long shoots or parties or lying awake in bed filled with a nameless dread that had been plaguing him for the past week. It got worse every time he thought about his LA house, huge and gleaming and empty.

"Yeah," he said. "I guess we were."

Rusty had rented them a limo.

Arthur stared. It was speckled with snow, which had started up again while he was at the party. It looked entirely out of place sitting on the side of the cramped road in front of Musgrove Inn. Like something from another life.

Arthur stood there until his tail started to go numb. Then he climbed into the backseat.

Rusty looked up from his phone. "Hey! Look what I got! You arrived with a bang, might as well go out on one, right?"

"Right," Arthur agreed mindlessly, dropping his suitcase into the roomy footwell.

Rusty went back to scrolling, slouching back into his seat as the limo started down the road. "Can't wait to get on that fucking plane. I'm gonna pass out the second my head hits the seat, I know it. Also, hey, look what I found at the party..."

He rummaged in his pocket.

Arthur cut him off before he could reveal it. "Why'd you say that, back at Sour Claw?"

Rusty paused, hand stilling in his pocket. "Huh?"

"At the bar," Arthur explained. "I wanted to fix things with Emma. You asked me why."

Rusty frowned. Just for a second. Then his expression cleared out, something that Arthur would've done his best to ignore two weeks ago.

"Dunno," Rusty said. "I started drinking with that vampire and orc duo after that. I don't remember much about that night."

He laughed. It was too desperate.

Arthur was annoyed by how shitty he was at faking it. "Don't bullshit me, Rust. Don't sit there and tell me what you think I want to hear. Just tell me the truth."

Rusty's mouth hung open. Arthur had never talked to him like that before. He didn't talk to *anyone* like that outside of a scene. Arthur was widely known as the sweetest guy in Hollywood. No dirty secrets, no hotel workers signing NDAs to hide that he screamed at them for not folding a towel correctly, no outrageous behavior even at his wildest parties. If Arthur had something to say he thought someone wouldn't like, he hid it in something so pretty the person barely noticed what was inside.

"I just..." Rusty said slowly. He let out another thin laugh. "Arthur. Come on, buddy. She doesn't matter! She's a childhood fling, who cares if she's unhappy? She's not part of your life. She's already gone, man. Speck in the distance. Sure, you had to look at her for a few weeks, but now you're leaving, and you never have to see her again."

Something flicked Arthur in the chin. He looked down and saw his fucking tail at it again, swishing agitatedly as Rusty pulled something out of his pocket.

"Here," Rusty said. "Found this on the drinks table."

Arthur held his tail in his lap and looked over.

Rusty was holding out his sunglasses. The same ones he'd been wearing when he strode back into Claw Haven, ready for two weeks of uncomfortable nostalgia before he cruised back out. Ready for his real life to continue. To leave his hometown behind him forever, never looking back. He hadn't thought about Emma. Scratch that—

he'd tried *so hard* not to think about Emma. He had assumed she would avoid him, and that it would be for the best. He'd assumed that he'd see her in passing on the street and they'd both pretend to ignore each other. He hadn't expected a bone-deep urge to rise in him the second he saw her. Hadn't expected to see that old rage and want to peel it back to expose that beautiful heart underneath. Hadn't expected her to kiss him in his cabin or in the street in front of the house they had been planning to buy. Hadn't expected to knot her, to long for her, to fall for her all over again.

The welcome sign was coming up. Arthur hadn't seen the other side of the new sign before.

You are now leaving Claw Haven, it declared. *Come back if you're looking for some peace and quiet.*

The limo slid past. Arthur twisted in his seat to watch the sign get smaller and smaller.

"Hey," Rusty said.

Arthur looked at him. Rusty was still holding out the sunglasses expectantly. He was trying to look concerned. But the matter remained that Rusty was never a good actor. Especially now, his smile dimming with every second Arthur stayed silent.

Arthur sighed, letting his shoulders drop in a way he hadn't allowed in a long, long time.

"Rust," he said. "We need to talk."

FIFTEEN

Emma woke up to the annoying and beloved jingle her parents used to wake her up for every teenage Christmas she ever had.

"That was terrible," she said as she answered the call. "Shouldn't have let you talk me into that. I almost threw my pillow at it on instinct."

Her parents laughed. They had gotten good at ducking the pillows Emma would throw upon being woken up by their very loud and deliberately bad singing.

Emma checked the time and groaned. "It's 8 a.m., guys! What time is it over there?"

"Time for you to wake up," they chorused in creepy parental unison.

Emma shuffled up against the bedframe, smiling sleepily. Her parents were still in their PJs in their hotel room with the light on, which told her absolutely nothing about what time it was there.

"How was your night?" Bitsey asked.

"It was…" Emma stopped, her heart squeezing in her chest as she thought back to Arthur's lost gaze on her as she turned to leave. He hadn't chased after her. She was relieved and *so* goddamn disappointed. If he'd tried to ask her to come to LA again, or even just asked for one more tryst, it would've made things so much harder.

Emma cleared her throat. She didn't want to think about that.

"You guys want to hear something really stupid?" she asked. "They took *The Harpy's Holiday* off Netflix."

Bitsey groaned. "What are we going to watch on New Year's?"

"Right?" Emma said. "It's so dumb! Let us have this one thing!"

Her parents laughed. Then they both sat there, waiting. Shooting each other not-so-subtle looks. Trying to get the other one to ask.

Emma sighed. "The party was *fine*, okay? I left pretty fast."

"At least you went," Glen said immediately.

"Right," Bitsey agreed. "There's never any harm in showing up."

Emma chewed her lip. She wanted to argue there fucking *had* been harm in showing up, that she would've been better off staying home. That last conversation with Arthur had been awful, all longing and desperation from both sides. She felt like she'd been pried open with a can opener. She felt *exposed*, like a raw nerve, liable to flinch at the lightest touch. There was a *reason* why she'd gone with anger for so long. It was easier. Dealing with this crap was messy and complicated, and it *hurt*.

"Emma?" Bitsey asked. "Are you okay?"

Emma opened her mouth to say she was fine, shut up, and move on to presents now.

Instead, she swallowed and said, "I think so. I don't know if I ever, like, *mourned* him properly. I just got mad and didn't process any of the shit under it. Turns out I'm really fucking sad! I feel so *stupid*. I really thought we were gonna—"

Her voice broke. She put the phone down, giving her parents a lovely view of the blank ceiling.

"It's so stupid," she croaked. "We broke up when we were kids! I can't believe I'm still so fucked up over him! He swans into town and talks to me a few times, and I'm just—I'm *gone*. It's so *easy* with him; I hate how easy he makes it."

She sniffed, wiping her face on her sleeve.

Bitsey's throat cleared uncomfortably. "You can keep going, hon. We'll listen to whatever you have to say."

Emma rolled her wet eyes and picked the phone back up. "No, I refuse to do this right now. I'll talk about it later. Right now I just wanna have a good time opening gifts with my parents. Where's the gift I gave you before you got on the ship?"

"Right," Glen said. "About that..."

"We didn't want to say," Bitsey said over him. "But it seems to have gotten lost in transit."

"We bought ourselves something to make up for it," Glen added. "You can pay us back."

Emma laughed wetly. "Shit! How much was it?"

"*So* expensive," they said in one.

Emma's next laugh was cut short by a knock on the front door.

She frowned. "One second, someone's at the door. Probably the neighbor needing a snow shovel again. I don't know how she keeps losing it. *Don't* open anything."

She set her phone on her pillow and headed for the front door.

"If you want the shovel," she said as she opened it. "You'll have to get it yourself; I'm not putting shoes..."

She trailed off.

Arthur waved. He was wearing a scarf and a deeply ugly Christmas sweater, and he was very notably *not* in LA like he should've been.

"What are you doing here?" Emma whispered.

Arthur pulled at his awful Christmas sweater. He was so close Emma could reach out and touch him. *Here*, her mind kept screaming. He was *here* in Claw Haven, standing on her ramp with his wings pulled tight and his tail swishing harder than she'd ever seen it.

"I was kind of hoping to start with Merry Christmas." Arthur smiled rakishly. It lasted maybe a second before fading into something so real and nervous that Emma's heart skipped a beat.

"I want to show you something," he continued. "Come with me."

"What?" Emma stumbled back, unable to stop an incredulous laugh. "No! Why are you here?"

His wings twitched. His tail wound around his own leg like he was a little kid. Then his tail jerked away and his wings loosened. Emma watched him try to pull the mask back up and then... stop. His wings stayed tense. His tail kept fidgeting.

"I didn't want you to spend Christmas alone," he said in a rush.

Emma's throat tightened. She swallowed hard. "I'm... I'm going to the Musgrove Inn later. You didn't— I— What about your flight?"

He shrugged. "Missed it."

"When's your new one?"

"Haven't booked one," Arthur said simply. "Can I please show you something?"

Do not read into this, Emma told herself. But it was pretty fucking hard not to read too much into your movie star ex missing his flight back home to show up on Christmas Day. Hope was filling her to her fingertips even as she stubbornly fought it back.

He gazed down at her, eyes so soft and golden she had to stop herself from swaying forward into his arms and his truly godawful sweater. It had *baubles*.

"Give me a second," she said. "I have to go hang up on my parents."

"Oh," Arthur said. "Damn. I didn't mean to—"

Emma closed the door and ran back to her room, where her parents were arguing idly about who would win in a fight, cavemen or astronauts, an argument that had started when Emma was twelve and had never been won.

"Gotta go, sorry, love you, talk later," she hissed, ending the call.

She got dressed in a hurry and ran back to the door, throwing it open to find Arthur pulling up another hasty smile.

"You can keep talking to them if you want," he said.

She shook her head. "Do you remember calling them a few years ago on New Year?"

He blinked at her, baffled. "Did I?"

"Tell you later." She stepped out onto the ramp. "Are we walking?"

He paused. Then he held out his arms. He didn't look smug and expectant like last time. His open arms were a question rather than a statement.

Emma wound her arms around his neck. He slid his arm under her knee and behind her shoulders. There was an incredible, heart-wrenching moment where she was just lying there in his warm grip, his wings shielding her from the snow. Then his wings flared open, and they took off.

The wind was freezing. Emma barely felt it.

She buried her face in Arthur's fur, inhaling his heady scent. Less fur cream, more plain Arthur. He'd even let his mane get a little frizzy, she noticed as he flew them toward the middle of town. She toyed with the strands, marveling. What the hell had changed last night to make him ditch his flight?

He landed in the middle of a snowy street.

"It's not perfect," he said. "But it's a start."

Emma stared. She stepped onto the icy concrete, eyes filling as she took it in.

It was the house. *Their* house, wisteria hanging off the porch railings, which were painted the exact shade of white that they'd agreed on when they were teenagers. The walls of the actual house were still chipped and the garden was still overgrown. But it was recognizably theirs.

Emma turned to him. "*How*?"

"Jackson helped." Arthur laughed nervously. "I paid him a *lot*. Good ol' birdhouse guy. Luckily, dragons can see in the dark; *I* had to get a flashlight."

Emma gaped at him. "Arthur. What the *hell*?"

She didn't mean for it to come out as pissed off. But she was so dazed with shock, a hundred possibilities running through her mind at once.

"I bought it," Arthur said. "Last night. The mayor was happy to let me take it off his hands and start fixing it up for real."

"Why?" Emma whispered.

"Because—" Arthur started. His tail swished anxiously. "Because I've never been so complete until I saw you again. LA is bright, it's fun, it's *distracting*. But it's really fucking empty. No one sees me. Not like you."

Emma felt a tear spill down her cheek. She scrubbed at it, fighting against a sob and a cheek-burning smile.

"What about your job, Mr. Fucking-movie-star?"

"I can cut back," he replied immediately. "A movie every few years."

Emma laughed. "Every few *years*? You'd get so bored!"

"I'd learn how to make coffee," Arthur tried. "I'd carry drinks, work in sales. I don't know. I've heard I can be very convincing."

Emma shivered. She'd only grabbed two layers on her way out.

Arthur hesitated. Then he wrapped her up in his wings, pulling her devastatingly close.

"I love you," he said. "I never stopped. You didn't hold me back, you just—you *held* me, and I'm sorry I didn't realize that's what I needed before I ruined everything. I'll spend every day of the rest of my life making it up to you if you let me."

Emma heard herself giggle, another tear dripping down her cheek. "I feel like I'm in a movie."

His wings tightened, pressing them tighter together.

"You're not. This isn't—" Arthur growled. "I'm not bullshitting, Emma. There's no script. Just me."

He stopped, panting. Gone was the movie star who had swaggered into town two weeks before Christmas. His ears were flat against his head, his wings stiff, and his blunt claws dug into his hands. His mane was scruffy and he didn't smell like anything but himself.

"Emma," he said again.

She reached up. There was something wet on his furry cheek.

"I've never seen you cry before," Emma said. "Not for real."

He huffed a wet laugh. "I can do it on command! Want to know how?"

She nodded.

"I think about you," he confessed. "Walking away from you. The only time I ever let myself properly think about you was during a scene. That look I'm so well known for, the one that gets me all the romantic leading roles, it's because I'm thinking about you."

It was the kind of line that would come at the end of a movie. The kind that would make Emma swoon, despite all her cynical trappings. But she looked up at him and knew it wasn't an act. This was Arthur. Her Arthur, no act involved. He'd come back to her, older and wiser, hoping for something to change him. Just like she'd been waiting for something to change her.

She gripped his terrible Christmas sweater. "Buying me a house is going to be really hard to top."

"What?"

"Next Christmas," she explained. "It's going to be pretty impossible to top this."

He stared at her, a slow smile spreading over his face.

"We can brainstorm," he said.

She dragged him down by his Christmas sweater baubles.

His mouth opened with a grateful groan. His wings tightened around her until all she could see were feathers. Feathers and him, looking down at her with that soft, impossible expression that always belonged to her.

SPECIAL THANKS

Thank you so much for reading CHRISTMAS WITH A CHIMERA, the second novella set in snowy Claw Haven.

If you liked this book, you might also want to read a full-length Claw Haven book - Accidentally Wedded To A Werewolf, is available on Amazon, B&N, and KU.

Get exciting Claw Haven updates by signing up to my newsletter at isabelletaylorauthor.com.

Acknowledgments

Let's hear it for the publishing team!

Edward Giordano, formatter extraordinaire, my fabulous editor Naomi Darling, Nikolai Espera aka @nikespera.png on Insta for the awesome cover, my typographer, Laya Rose, and last but not least, my fantastic beta reader, Matthew (Dragon68).

About the Author

Isabelle Taylor writes cozy, spicy monster romance books for adults. She works in a bookstore in New Zealand and has a Creative Writing Masters from the International Institute of Modern Letters.

She can be found on Instagram and Tiktok @isabelletaylorauthor.

instagram.com/isabelletaylorauthor

tiktok.com/@isabelletaylorauthor

Also by I. S. Belle

I. S. Belle

LGBT+ Young Adult Fiction

BABYLOVE SERIES

BABYLOVE

SUGARSNAP

SWEETHEARTS

ZOMBABE

ZOMBABE

HONEYBLOODS SERIES

HONEYBLOODS

HONEYBITES

HONEYCRAVES

GIRLS NIGHT

GIRLS NIGHT